The journey had begun uneventfully.
No sooner had they touched French
soil than it seemed they were rolling
on towards the South, where some of
France's loveliest scenery awaited them.
France, Spain, Portugal. Although none
of it would be new to Angus, all of it
would be full of memories. He was to see
it all again – and this time, he wouldn't
be paying to see it; he was actually being
paid. Everything, he felt, was in hand.
The success of the trip was assured.
Nothing could go wrong.

And for twenty-four hours, nothing did.

Also by Elizabeth Cadell

COME BE MY GUEST
SHADOWS ON THE WATER
CANARY YELLOW
THE CORNER SHOP
THE YELLOW BRICK ROAD
THE CUCKOO IN SPRING
BRIDAL ARRAY
SPRING GREEN

and published by Corgi Books

Elizabeth Cadell

The Green Empress

CORGI BOOKS
A DIVISION OF TRANSWORLD PUBLISHERS LTD
A NATIONAL GENERAL COMPANY

THE GREEN EMPRESS
A CORGI BOOK o 552 09207 X

Originally published in Great Britain
by Hodder & Stoughton Limited

PRINTING HISTORY
Hodder & Stoughton edition published 1958
Corgi edition published 1973

Copyright © 1958 by Elizabeth Cadell

This book is set in Intertype Plantin

Corgi Books are published by Transworld Publishers Ltd.,
Cavendish House, 57-59 Uxbridge Road,
Ealing, London W.5.
Made and printed in Great Britain by
Hunt Barnard Printing Ltd., Aylesbury, Bucks.

The Green Empress

CHAPTER 1

'Do you,' asked Sir Claud finally, 'feel confident to undertake the work?'

There was anxiety in his voice, but there was anguish in the look he directed towards the large young man seated at the other side of the bare, highly-polished desk.

The young man returned the gaze politely, but with unruffled calm, and Sir Claud, running a distracted hand over his sparse grey hairs, leaned back in his chair and tried to discover what was making him hesitate on the brink of decision.

He had done all he could. He had granted the rare privilege of a personal interview, and at the beginning of it had put the candidate through a stiff verbal examination. He had found him alert, well-informed and intelligent; he also fulfilled the other requirements of the Company: his background was impeccable, his looks pleasant, his voice and bearing good. But in the later stages of the interview, when Sir Claud had spoken at some length of the heavy responsibility involved in working for the Company, when he had stressed the necessity of upholding its high standards, he had felt that something was missing in the young man's manner. Something was missing, but he could not decide, he could not define exactly what it was. There was polite attention; the young man had listened to what was being said to him with a quietness and ease of manner and –

And that was it!

There, Sir Claud told himself, there was the flaw. There was the fault, elusive, intangible, that he had sensed but failed to identify. It was this that had worried him: this ease, this calm, almost this coolness of manner. It could spring only from a conviction that a thorough knowledge of detail was sufficient qualification for the post. This young man, satisfactory in all other respects, obviously considered that efficiency was enough.

Efficiency was not enough. Sir Claud, in a last effort to drive this fact home, leaned forward and spoke earnestly.

'You fully understand, Mr Graham, what you are undertaking?'

'Perfectly, sir,' said Angus, and marvelled at his own self-control. For forty minutes he had been fighting a strong impulse to rise and inform this tedious old man that there was no need to go on droning out instructions; he had grasped the details and he could do the job on his head. If he couldn't conduct a busload of travellers across country that he knew like the palm of his hand, if he was incapable of acting for a short time as combined courier, steward and nursemaid to a collection of mobile millionaires, he must indeed be as weak-witted as this old man appeared to find him. He –

Attention, Angus, he warned himself. *The old gentleman's off again.*

'You do understand' – Sir Claud enunciated each word slowly and clearly – 'you do understand that you are not – let me repeat this emphatically – you are not a courier?'

'The duties, sir,' Angus could not help pointing out, 'are those of a courier.'

'Perhaps.' The old man shifted forward in his seat and seemed to be trying to project his doubts, his uneasiness, across the desk. 'But I have been at pains throughout this interview to make you see that we are not to be classed as a mere Travel Agency, and that our young men are emphatically not couriers. They accompany our travellers, they are at hand to point out, if required, points of interest on the journey; they are prepared to help or to advise. They act as liaison officers between our clients and . . . Yes, that is the term: they are liaison officers. They are not, definitely not, couriers.'

I thought he was saying ham, Angus told himself wearily, *and he was saying ham all the time.* With an effort, he injected a note of solemnity into his voice.

'A liaison officer. I quite see that there is more than a shade of difference, sir,' he said.

He saw the instant relief and pleasure in the old man's face and reproached himself for not having put him at his ease earlier. He had known what was lacking in his own manner, but he had been reluctant to repair the omission; what Sir Claud had expected, had awaited, was respect amounting to awe for the Company, and this Angus had been unwilling to grant. It was, in his opinion, no more than a firm that specialised in giving rich travellers rich treatment, and he himself was nothing more, he considered, than a mobile wet-nurse. But if getting the job meant humouring the Company's head and founder, he was prepared to humour him.

8

He needed the job, he reminded himself. He needed it badly. It would fill in more than a month: a week going, a week or two there, a week returning. It would pay him well and it would give him a look, perhaps a last look, at the Europe he loved so much. He wanted the job. If getting it meant putting on this I-hope-I-am-worthy act, he was prepared to put it on.

'I understand perfectly, sir,' he said.

Sir Claud smiled.

'I am glad. Our Company is, in many respects, an unusual organisation. In the first place, we are Government-sponsored. We do not arrange travel for the ordinary tourist, and we do not take people on sight-seeing tours. Our passengers, as you now know, are very often people high in the service of this or other nations. You asked, with some point, why, if they are going on important missions, they do not go by air. The answer is that the mission may be important, but it is perhaps not urgent, and so they avail themselves of our service, which carries them in the utmost comfort and which also allows them a choice of route. It is this that separates us so widely from other firms which undertake to conduct travellers across Europe, and it is because we offer such specialised service that I hesitated before giving you this assignment. Our young men are specialists. In their hands, throughout the journey, rests the reputation of the firm. I am sure that you, with your attainments, will uphold our high standards.'

Angus bowed. He had not up to now heard his knowledge of languages referred to as attainments. Perhaps there was something else that he could do that for the moment had slipped his mind. Navigation? He could dock a battleship – or he had once been able to. Perhaps if he tried today . . . Two years was a long time. Perhaps he'd been foolish to let himself drift out of Naval circles; perhaps if he'd steeled himself to go on seeing his friends, if he'd . . . if, in fact, he told himself grimly, if he'd taken the whole thing in a tougher spirit, perhaps he wouldn't be sitting here now listening to this long-winded old man telling him how to be a courier without calling himself one.

Depression settled on him, and he shook it off. The past was nobody's fault, and the future was in Canada and perhaps he'd grow to like it. If he wasn't to end up as an Admiral, he might end by becoming an oil magnate. And if he had to leave England, if he had to face up to the fact that he could not see much more of his beloved Spain or France or Italy, perhaps he'd find compensation in Canada. Perhaps. And in the meantime, believe it or not, old Sir Claud was still talking.

' – and you will forgive me when I say that I hesitated only because we have never before used a young man whom we have not trained ourselves. But Mr Sealing's accident created an emergency, and I am grateful to you for filling his place. At the same time, I must point out that without his assurance that you could act successfully in his stead, without his promise to brief you, without your own fluency in the required languages, we could not have brought ourselves to give you the appointment.'

So the job was his. Good old Wax, thought Angus gratefully, to think of him and to recommend him . . . and not to put him off beforehand by telling him that the whole show looked like falling backwards under a sense of its own importance.

Sir Claud rose, and Angus rose with him and wondered if any cubits had been added to his stature; he had sat down a plain Scotsman and had risen a cou . . . a liaison officer.

While they awaited the young man into whose care Angus was to be consigned, Sir Claud touched warily upon a new theme.

'Mr Sealing tells me that you are going to Canada.'

'Yes, sir. I've got a job with an oil firm in Edmonton.'

'I see. I'm sorry you had to leave the Navy. That was bad luck.'

'Yes.' Angus had nothing to add to the monosyllable. It was bad luck. Yes.

'If you prove yourself in this assignment . . . of course, if you are committed to the Canadian job . . . but you seem to be our type and there may possibly be an opening . . . '

Sir Claud's voice trailed into silence; he had conveyed what he wished to convey.

'Thank you, sir,' said Angus formally.

Then he was walking across the expanse of beautiful carpet and passing through heavy oak doorways in the wake of the young man from Mobility. There were four departments to which he had to go for final instructions, but so smooth were the workings of the firm, that he found himself, in less than an hour, standing in the late May sunshine outside the firm's premises in Hanover Square, a sheaf of papers and documents in a folder under his arm.

Twenty-four hours. He had twenty-four hours before joining the coach and leaving the country.

He spent two of them at the Nursing Home with his friend Wax Sealing.

'Thank you for putting in a word for me,' he said.

'I didn't put in a word; I merely put in your name,' Wax told him. 'You didn't think old Claud would hire you before he'd looked you over personally, did you?'

'Did you tell him I'd been invalided out of the Navy?'

'I've just told you: I told him nothing, except your name and your age: twenty-eight. After that, he set his spies in motion. With the cargoes we carry, he felt he couldn't afford to take any chances. He'll have ferreted out your history from the moment you emerged from your mother's you-know-what. If he'd discovered anything discreditable, he wouldn't have interviewed you.'

'He held back a bit at first. It was – '

' – your damned casual manner, I bet. You've got this unhurried, untroubled air and – '

'If you look untroubled, you reassure the customers, surely?'

'You probably made old Claud feel that you hadn't got the hang of the thing. He may look like a dried twig, but he's built up an amazing organisation. They made him a Knight and before he's through they'll make him a Baron and he'll deserve it. In my opinion, which admittedly is a biased one, he's a pioneer. What's more, he gives absolute value for money.'

'Doesn't any other Travel Company do the same?'

'Not in the same way. Other companies have stated routes, and you take 'em or leave 'em. What Sir Claud does is assemble groups of people who've got to get somewhere in not too great a hurry, and see that they get there in superlative comfort. If they want to do a bit of sight-seeing on the way, there's nothing to prevent them – but the sight-seeing's incidental. When they stop for the night, it isn't at hotels crammed with lesser travellers; Claud's bought up places all along the routes, and turned them into hotels for his own passengers. Some of them are in out-of-the-way little beauty spots and – '

'What do the passengers do at the out-of-the-way beauty spots?'

'They relax, mostly. Remember that the majority of them are seasoned travellers; they've done the round of churches and museums and monuments. Now they're merely driving to their destination as comfortably as they'd do in their own cars – only without the trouble of making the arrangements themselves. Naturally, Claud makes them pay plenty.'

'Nobody told me the actual amount. What do they pay?'

Wax told him, and Angus clutched the side of the bed for support.

'B-but for that amount,' he brought out, when he could speak, 'they could – '

' – do the trip several times with some other Company. Quite. But they don't, because they've discovered that we give them something rather special. Your job is to leave them strictly alone unless they ask you for anything. You do the rounds, of course, to see they're happy. And you travel on equal terms; that is, you lunch and dine with them and sleep in equal comfort. We're not couriers – remember?'

'But – '

'If I know Claud, he's given you Ferdy Brewer as driver. Ferdy's one of the soundest men they've got and he'll be able to help you if you need him.'

'But – '

'What's worrying you?'

'The set-up. It all looks too elaborate.'

'It is elaborate. Nothing's left to chance.'

'What does Government-sponsored mean?'

Wax grinned.

'That was thrown in to impress you. There's a certain amount of truth in the claim: we do carry high-ups going on missions. For example, you've got Lord Lorrimer; he's going to take the Chair at that international whatever-it-is in Lisbon.' He paused. 'Incidentally, isn't he the father of your Naval buddy?'

'Yes.'

'I'd forgotten. Well, you'll have his daughter on board, too. I suppose you know her?'

Angus shook his head.

'No. I met her years ago, when she was about seventeen, but I don't think we've met since. Her brother – '

' – didn't subscribe to that silly scheme of uniting kid sister with best friend? He was dead right. I wish I'd been as firm with my own sister. She's a pretty enough girl, but every time she wants to make up a party, she makes a grab at my friends. It gives them a trapped feeling, and it makes things awkward all round.'

'Well.' Angus rose. 'Thanks for the job.'

'It's a good job,' said Wax, 'and it's better paid than most. It's interesting, and up to a point it's varied. But somehow . . . I don't see you in it permanently. You were too long in the Navy. You'd get cramp. You need something wider.'

'Canada's wide enough, they tell me.'

'But what about all your languages? The Navy can't be the only show for which you could interpret?'

'I tried jobs in this country. My God, how I tried . . . You know how much I wanted to stay in Europe. But when I went looking for jobs, I discovered that every third man or woman speaks nine languages, or a dozen, or fourteen – not counting the Hindu dialects. Linguists come at three a penny.' He smiled down at his friend. 'I daresay I can take a trip to Quebec now and then, to brush up my French.'

'You wouldn't,' Wax asked him, 'like to take out any of these lovely nurses on your last night?'

'We'll both take them out when I get back.'

'Well, so long. Give my love to Ferdy. And take care of yourself, and remember our slogan.'

'I've never heard it.'

'Neither have I,' confessed Wax. 'But if we've got one, it's to the effect that however leisurely the trip, the coach always gets there on time. See to it.'

'I will.'

Angus went back to his rooms and extracted the papers and documents from the folder. The job, he concluded, wasn't as all-important as it was made out to be, but it was a job and he was glad to have it and he wanted to do it well.

On the following morning, he made his way to the firm's headquarters. Parked outside was a small coach painted a quiet shade of green. On its sides appeared, unobtrusively, the words *Green Empress*.

His eyes on the vehicle, Angus felt for the first time a stir of interest in his assignment. She was the colour of the sea and she had a ship's long, graceful lines. His feeling of being a herdsman lessened and gave way to pleasure at the thought of boarding the *Empress* and seeing from the wide windows some of the views he knew and liked so well. Whatever the kind or quality of the passengers, he would find pleasure, in between his spells of duty, in storing pictures of the passing scenes in his mind, to draw upon the hoard in years to come.

A stout, middle-aged man in dark-green uniform stood beside the coach. His bearing was as formal as Sir Claud would have wished, but when Angus approached, he addressed him with friendly ease.

'You'll be Mr Graham, sir?'

'Yes. You're – '

'Brewer, sir. Ferdinand Brewer. Ferdy to all you young gentlemen. New to the job, aren't you, sir?'

'As a matter of fact, I'm only filling in for Mr Sealing.'

'So I heard, sir. Been in the firm myself for close on eight years – ever since it was started, sir.' He stroked his greying moustache. 'I've taken these *Empresses* a few thousand miles.'

'Do you stick to the same route most of the time?'

'No, sir; they shift us round. If you want to be put right on any little point while we're on the way, sir, I'll be glad to help you.'

'Thank you.' He glanced at his watch. 'Ten more minutes. Do the passengers arrive punctually?'

'To the minute, as a rule, sir.' He nodded towards the coach. 'Seen the inside, sir?'

'No.'

'Take a look,' advised Ferdy. 'Neat jobs, they are. And to drive . . . ' He drew a long breath of satisfaction. 'Just purr along, they do.' He opened the door and waved a hand as large as a spade. 'Take a look, sir.'

Angus stepped in and stood looking round him, and as he took in the details of the coach's interior, he seemed to feel Sir Claud beside him, glowing with pride – a pride that Angus, at that moment, felt to be justified.

There were ten seats, built on an armchair design. They were set singly, five on each side of the coach; they were upholstered in pale grey leather and embodied the latest ideas of elegance and comfort. A lever released each chair, allowing it to swivel in whatever direction the occupant wished to face. The space between the seats was ample, and beside each passenger was a small locker, built into the side of the coach.

At the rear were three compartments. The lower half of the central one was a cupboard for coats, umbrellas and other impedimenta; above was a neat cocktail cabinet. On the left was a tiny but beautifully-fitted Powder Room; on the right, the gentlemen's washroom.

'Neat, isn't it, sir?' commented Ferdy, from the door.

Angus wanted to say that it was much more than neat, but a glance at his watch told him that the passengers were due. He stepped off the coach and prepared to check them as they came aboard.

As Ferdy had predicted, they were punctual. One by one, they gave up their numbered cards and, boarding the coach, made their way to their allotted seats. Soon, they were settled; their cases were in the luggage compartments, Ferdy was at the wheel, and Angus was seated in the place reserved for him – a glass-enclosed compartment with sliding doors in a central position in front of the passengers. Beside his own seat was an empty one which could be used by the passengers as an observation seat.

They were moving. With the silence and steadiness of a ship leaving the quay, they were making their way through the streets, heading towards the Channel and the ferry on which the *Green Empress* would cross to France.

The journey had begun.

Nothing, Angus found, had been left out. A mirror, strategically placed, gave him a view of the passengers seated behind him. He could observe them, identify them; soon it would be his duty to move among them down the spacious central corridor to make his first contact with them.

With mounting interest, he let his eyes roam over his charges. They were studying the small, printed passenger lists that had been placed on each seat. Angus glanced down at his own plan and read the names upon it. They sounded impressive.

Mr F. Brewer

Mr Angus Graham

1. Lord Lorrimer	6. Miss C. Seton
2. Mr Lionel Yule	7. Mr Stanton Holt
3. The Honble Angela Clunes	8. Sir Maurice Tarrant, Bt
	9. Mrs Denby-Warre
4. Mrs Zoller	10. Admiral Sir Rodney Peterson
5. Mr Zoller	

Angus studied them. He had no difficulty in recognising Lord Lorrimer, at whose house he had been, during his Naval days, a frequent guest. He did not think that Lord Lorrimer would recognise him, for on the occasions on which his son's Naval friends had held parties at the house, he and his wife had tactfully absented themselves.

Mr Zoller was also easy to recognise, for he appeared regularly in the newspapers; his donations to charity, though generous, were not given without publicity.

The Admiral was vaguely familiar. Angus groped in his mind to discover where he had seen him before. The occasion came back to him, and he moved his gaze to Angela Clunes, daughter of Lord Lorrimer and sister of the gay – often too gay – Oliver Clunes.

She was looking out of the window, and he could see only her profile. She seemed prettier than he remembered, but his memory of her, he admitted, was hazy. Studying her, he decided that she was a little too fair; he preferred black, glossy hair and round black eyes. He could see, from this angle, little resemblance to her brother.

His eyes went to the man seated in front of her: her father's secretary, Lionel Yule. He and she would make a handsome pair, he mused, if ever they made a pair. On the whole, he hoped that they wouldn't, for at a first glance, he felt that he would award Mr Yule more marks for deportment than for charm. From the frequent glances he was giving over his shoulder, it was easy to see that Angela occupied a large part of his mind, but Angus hoped that she would look further before making a choice. Perhaps, he reflected, she would marry Yule out of kindness. Women were like that. Take his own case: nobody had shown any great eagerness to marry him when he had a good, steady job as a Naval lieutenant, but put him in a rugger accident and get him thrown out on his ear, and women flocked. Kind, but mistaken.

On an impulse, he rose and stepped into the main part of the coach. It was not the scheduled time for his tour of the passengers, but he had a strong desire to hear as well as see them; to interview rather than to view.

He bent over Lord Lorrimer in what he hoped was the correct steward manner, and wondered whether it would be in order to ask how Oliver's wedding had gone off. It had taken place last week, and Angus had found an excuse for refusing to be best man and for not going to the wedding. He could forget the past more easily, he found, by avoiding Naval occasions.

Confining himself to a routine enquiry regarding Lord Lorrimer's comfort, he found that he had a few moments to wait for a reply: Lord Lorrimer's mind was far away. Presently his lean, handsome face came round to Angus's, and he made a visible effort to recall himself to the present.

'Oh. Oh yes, thank you. I'm very comfortable, thanks – as usual. This is my seventh *Empress* trip, you know.'

Mr Yule was also comfortable, but he was not communicative; he seemed to wish to remind Angus that he, too, was not doing the trip for fun; he was on duty.

'I wonder,' he asked, 'if you'd be so good as to keep this despatch case under lock and key? It has some rather important papers in it. I shall need them from time to time, but I would prefer not to keep them in this locker.'

Angus, placing the case in the cupboard at the rear of the coach, went back to assure Mr Yule that the matter would have his undivided attention throughout the journey.

And so, he thought as he bent over her, would Angela Clunes. A near view of her was a heady experience. Alabaster skin, a mouth soft and pink and curved, and the stimulating surprise of eyes not blue, to match her fairness, but dark brown velvet. Like that irritating heroine of Galsworthy's, Angus recalled, who spent the entire book shrinking – but this girl didn't look as though she would shrink from anything. Her glance had a directness he liked, and her manner combined qualities not often found together: liveliness and a certain dignity. Remembering her brother's infrequent and by no means complimentary references to her in recent years, Angus marvelled at the blindness of his friend.

Yes, she was comfortable. Yes, thank you, she could manage the window very well: open that way, shut that way; thank you. No, this wasn't her first *Empress* trip; it was her second, but surely he remembered that she was Oliver Clunes' sister? Wasn't it extraordinary, after all these years, that they should meet like this? Wasn't it awfully –

At this point, the chair in front began a slow but inexorable semicircle. The back of the seat gave place to the front of Mr Yule, from whose eyes a cold and suspicious glare pierced Angus's pleasant absorption. Straightening, he went on to Mrs Zoller, making a mental note that he must find out as soon as possible how much right Mr Yule had to break up meetings.

He found Mrs Zoller, at close range, less overpowering than he had anticipated. She was about forty: he had already taken in frankly dyed hair, flashing jewels and a generous exhibition of snowy bosom, but on approaching her, he found her large face placid and good-tempered. She raised blank, china-blue eyes and studied him with the open and unabashed scrutiny she had been giving her fellow passengers, and spoke in a voice with a strong German accent.

'You are new?'

'I'm deputising for somebody who was taken ill. Is this your first *Empress* trip?'

She gave a chuckle.

'My first? It is the fourth. He' – a wave of her hand indicated her husband, who was sitting behind her – 'comes by this way because it is comfortable, and he wishes, when he travels, to sleep all the time. Always, he sleeps. But he has not come for pleasure; it is only business. Who is this who is ill?'

'Mr Sealing.'

'Ah. Him I know. Tell him kind regards from me, please.'

'I will.' Angus left her and turned to her husband, to find that Mr Zoller had begun as he meant to go on: by sleeping.

That finished one side; now for the other. Beginning at the back, Angus approached the Admiral and saw that the years had made him more like the popular conception of a sea dog than ever: bluff, ruddy, keen-eyed, amply-proportioned. He gave Angus a puzzled look and seemed about to speak, when the chair in front did a smart semicircle and brought his sister, Mrs Denby-Warre, to face them.

There could hardly have been a greater contrast between two members of a family. The Admiral was all curves, his sister all angles; his face was smudged, hers etched. Her dress was severe, and so was the voice in which she addressed Angus.

'Young man, have you a large, clear map I could look at?'

He brought one from his compartment and gave it to her. She took it and thanked him, but before looking at it, she met the gaze of Mrs Zoller, seated on the other side of the coach. For only a moment, the two glances held, but in that moment Angus saw exchanged a brief but uncomplimentary message: Mrs Zoller clearly thought the other woman an extraordinary figure, while Mrs Denby-Warre made no secret of her opinion of a woman who wore diamonds in the morning and showed her bosom to strangers.

Somewhat shaken, Angus passed on to the next passenger, Sir Maurice Tarrant, who, with head screwed round, was awaiting his approach. About twenty-five, almost as fair as Angela Clunes, he had an uninhibited flow of conversation and an irrepressible manner that was already bringing a frown to the Admiral's brow. He greeted Angus, and in a voice he did not trouble to lower, informed him that this was his first trip on an *Empress* and that it seemed comfortable enough but that the average age of the passengers was too high to ensure a really amusing journey – and wasn't that Angela Clunes over there, and couldn't something be done to move people around a bit so as to allow her to, as it were, circulate?

Angus told him that the passengers were free to change their seats if they wished to do so, and passed on hoping that Sir Maurice would not prove too much of a handful on the journey.

Arriving at the next passenger, Mr Stanton Holt, he found him to be about forty, American, and of strong build. His manner was as free from self-consciousness as Maurice Tarrant's, but infinitely more restful. He studied Angus through large, horn-rimmed spectacles and then spoke in a slow drawl.

'I haven't used these coaches before,' he said. 'Would they carry something to drink?'

'I can give you a short drink,' Angus told him, 'before lunch or before dinner.'

'Fine, fine,' said Mr Holt approvingly. 'I don't overdo it, you understand, but' – he smiled engagingly – 'I like to do it. Would you,' he went on, 'ask the lady sitting in front of me if I could talk to her?'

Angus waited a moment, but there was not a quiver from the lady seated in front. Stepping forward, he bent over Miss Seton, only to find that bending was of no use, since she was wearing a hat that had been modelled from a giant mushroom. He could see slim ankles and expensive, high-heeled shoes, but nothing short of getting on his knees and gazing upward could have shown him her features.

'Miss Seton?'

She looked up. He found himself looking down at a woman in her late thirties, with a plain, broad face whose most compelling feature was a pair of warm, humorous, intelligent hazel eyes.

'I wonder,' asked Angus, 'if you would allow me to introduce Mr Stanton Holt to you?'

'That's me,' came from Mr Holt. 'If you could most kindly turn your chair around – '

Miss Seton, revolving slowly, came face to face with him and inclined her head.

'How do you do?'

'I'd do better if I could talk to you,' said Mr Holt frankly. 'I was going to tap you on the shoulder and ask if I could get to know you, but then I thought it might be kind of wiser if I waited and what you'd call observed the formalities. And now I hope we're acquainted?'

Miss Seton gave him a long, unhurried survey that ended in a smile.

'I admire your courage,' she said.

'Courage?'

She glanced up at Angus.

'You tell him,' she said.

'I think,' said Angus, translating, 'that Miss Seton means you've got courage because you've risked spoiling your journey by inviting somebody you don't know, and may later find uncongenial, to make friends with you. Am I right, Miss Seton?'

'Quite right,' she said.

'And that, I suppose,' observed Mr Holt, 'is the reason the British sit in trains and planes looking like they wished they were some place else?'

'On a short journey, why bother to talk to anybody?' asked Miss Seton. 'And on a long one . . . I've just pointed out the risk.'

'Well, that may be so,' allowed Mr Holt, 'but I always get kind of lonely when I leave home, and I had one experience I told myself I'd never repeat: I shared a cabin with a Britisher all the way from Southampton to New York, and all he ever said to me, the whole trip, was "Goodbye, ol' chap." '

'But think how *restful*!' said Miss Seton.

'Well, don't you be restful,' he implored. 'I liked the back of you and I like the front of you and if you'll only stay this way up, I'll be grateful and I hope I won't bother you. Will you let me ask Mr Graham to bring you a drink?'

Lord Lorrimer, overhearing, ordered sherry for himself, his secretary and his daughter. Mr Zoller stirred, opened small, shrewd eyes, fixed them unblinkingly on Angus and asked him if he had a pink chin.

'A – ?' began Angus, momentarily at a loss.

Mrs Zoller, translating indulgently, explained that what her husband wanted was a pink shin.

'Of course,' said Angus.

The Admiral also wanted gin. His sister wanted lemonade.

When Angus brought it to her, she took it with some suspicion.

'This is real lemon, I hope?'

'Real lemon,' he assured her.

'Not out of a bottle?'

'No. I cut a fresh lemon in half and squeezed it.'

'Oh, thank you. Thank you so much.' She sipped it and nodded. 'Delicious. My brother,' she went on, 'has been telling me that he has seen you before, and – '

'I'm on the temporary staff. I'm taking the place of a friend of mine.'

'And what happened to him?'

Angus smiled.

'He rescued a pretty girl's poodle from under a bus in Piccadilly.'

'And he was hurt?'

'Not by the bus. He got entangled in the poodle's lead, and landed awkwardly.'

'I see. Well, I hope you enjoy taking his place.'

'Thank you.'

He went back to his compartment feeling that they were, on the whole, a nice lot – with the possible exception of Maurice Tarrant, who might give a bit of trouble. Lord Lorrimer seemed to have something on his mind, he mused; only a small part of him seemed to be present; the rest was far away, and in not too happy a place. His secretary, and the despatch case, proved that he had work to do on the journey, but even heavy responsibility shouldn't give people that lost sort of look. And Lord Lorrimer had more reason than most to look happy; he had a pleasant and secure place in the world, a son who had just made a brilliant marriage and a daughter . . .

He brought his mind firmly away from the daughter. There was work to be done; he was not on a pleasure trip.

He looked out at the landscape. They were passing the Kent orchards; a month ago, he remembered, he had driven along this stretch of road and had seen on either side a glory of pink and white blossom. If he tried to tell his children, in years to come, about the Kent orchards in spring, would he have to translate his theme into a transatlantic idiom? Canada had her beauties, and he must learn to love them as he loved this land and the lands across the narrow strip of English Channel. Twenty-eight was young enough to be adaptable. His search for jobs since he left the Navy had been valuable time wasted, and he must go where the job was – and soon. He had already drawn too much upon his slender capital.

A sound behind him made him turn, and he saw that Angela Clunes was entering his little compartment. He rose to close the door behind her, and she settled herself in the observation seat and turned to him at once with a direct question.

'You don't remember me – or hardly at all, do you?'

He hesitated.

'It was a long time ago. I – '

'That's what you think. But you've seen me, off and on, at lots of places – only of course, not in your party. Oliver saw to that.'

'I remember you as a seventeen-year-old, but I – '

'I didn't expect any notice from you then, of course. No sub-lieutenant would dream of paying any attention to a woman under thirty. Since then, I've been trying to induce Oliver to bring us together, but he made me see how stinkingly humiliating it would be for any man to look as though he was foisting his sister on his friends. Why weren't you at his wedding?'

'I – '

' – have spent the time since you left the Navy carefully avoiding all Naval contacts. Well, you missed a good wedding. I was the chief bridesmaid and I looked heavenly and I did so wish you'd been there.' She turned in her seat to get a better view of him. 'Isn't it *amazing* that you're on this coach?'

'Well – '

'What I actually mean is, wouldn't you call it fate?'

Angus considered.

'No, I wouldn't,' he said at last.

'That's because you don't know all the facts. Do you realise that after all these years of trying to meet you face to face, as it were, and not succeeding, I get on a *Green Empress* and there you are? Now say it isn't fate.'

'Couldn't you just call it a happy coincidence?'

'No. My father promised, ages ago, to take me on this trip. I think he thought I'd feel miserable after Oliver got married, but I think he's feeling it more than I am. Don't you think he's looking dejected?'

'He didn't seem to be in good spirits.'

'You'd think he'd be glad that Oliver had settled down at last, but I think he misses him. He's been looking awfully miserable lately. He – What are you opening that map for?'

'Shouldn't you be taking an interest in the route?'

'You think I don't know where I'm going?'

He laughed.

'I'm on this coach in an official capacity, Miss Clunes, and so – '

'Miss . . . Miss Clunes!' she repeated in a slow, amazed voice. Her glance rested on him, intent and frowning. 'You're not suffering from some kind of inverted snobbishness, are you?'

'I hope not.'

'Then why address me as Miss Clunes, when you've been my brother's closest friend for years and years? You're going to see a lot of me during this trip, and it's no use starting off by behaving like a sheep-herder. Can't you take your mind off the job for a few minutes and talk to me in a calm, friendly way?'

Angus folded the map and spread his hands to indicate that he was at her disposal.

'That's better.' She smiled, and Angus had a startled conviction that a light had come on in the little compartment. 'Now we're friends, hm?'

'Of course, but – '

'Wait till I write and tell Oliver. I swore to him that I'd catch up with you one day – and I have.' She rose, and stood looking at him with a smile that made his head spin. He groped his way to the door and opened it for her. 'And you said it wasn't fate!' she said, as she left him.

Left alone, he sat down and tried to clear his head. He needed a little time. He must, he told himself firmly, sort this thing out and apply the brakes. How Oliver had managed to . . . But then, brothers were brothers. Did she always move at that pace? Was it his imagination, or had she left something of herself floating in the air around him, something soft and sweet and . . .

With a strong effort, he forced his mind back to his job. What was outside now? Hopfields. He'd read up hopfields last night, just in case. Nobody seemed to want to know anything about hopfields.

A cautious glance in his mirror showed him Angela back in her seat, writing busily. To Oliver, no doubt. And Oliver would laugh – a rude laugh, for he had been trying, lately, to get things on the old basis, and had not succeeded. And now his sister . . .

Almost to his relief, he saw Mrs Denby-Warre's angular figure approaching. He opened the door for her, and she lowered herself on to the chair beside him, sitting bolt upright and sternly resisting the comfort of the cushions.

'My brother doesn't know in the least where we're going,' she said, 'and so I came to ask you.'

She turned her long, sheep-like face to him expectantly, and he tried hard to remember that he was a courier and that a soft, scented breeze blowing through his glass cage could not possibly knock him off his balance. Pure imagination.

'We'll soon be crossing the Channel,' he told his questioner. 'Then we shall be – '

'My brother didn't want to come,' she confided, 'but I persuaded him – at last. I've been trying for years, you know, to get him to come on a little trip with me.'

'I hope he'll enjoy it.'

'I hope so too.' She sounded doubtful. 'I hope you'll be able to interest him in everything and make him forget his garden.'

'He likes his garden?'

'He lives for his garden. When he retired, he went to live in a small house in Somerset, and since then, all he has thought of is those two-and-a-half acres of garden. It shouldn't – should it? – take up a man's whole time?'

'Well, it's hard work and – '

'You were in the Navy, too, weren't you?'

'Yes.'

He waited for the inevitable questions, but to his relief they did not come.

'I'm the widow of an Admiral, the daughter of an Admiral and the sister of an Admiral,' she told him. 'I think that might be some kind of record.'

'It must be unusual.'

'I would so much have liked to be the mother of an Admiral, but I only had daughters.'

The noun was spoken with such undisguised disappointment, not to say disparagement, that Angus felt sorry for them.

'Is one permitted to ask questions about one's fellow-passengers? I was wondering who the Zollers were.'

'Mr Zoller's a millionaire, but I'm not quite sure what he does. He's travelling on business at the moment, his wife tells me.'

'I see.' She paused, and then spoke hesitatingly. 'You

won't think that I'm the sort of person who makes complaints, will you, but . . . I wonder if I may ask you to try and keep that young man under control ?'

'You mean – ?' asked Angus, who knew quite well.

'I mean Sir Maurice Tarrant. Could you ask him not to address my brother as Hornblower ?'

'I . . . It'll be difficult,' confessed Angus. 'I don't think he means any harm.'

'I knew his father many years ago; he was a quiet, careful man and he built up a large fortune. And now this young man is running through it with disgraceful speed. He's the only child, and his mother never had the slightest control over him. It's a pity they didn't put him into the Navy to learn a little discipline. Do you know that he has already called Lord Lorrimer "my dear fellow" several times ?'

'I don't think he means to offend people.'

'I wonder,' she said darkly. 'As you know, he's sitting in front of me – but that doesn't give him the right to join in the conversations I have with my brother. But when we were talking about somebody just now, I said to my brother: "I wish you had his flair" – and Maurice Tarrant turned round and said to me: "Nonsense, she's too young for him." Am I,' she demanded, 'to put up with that throughout the journey ?'

Angus, at a loss for an answer, was glad to find that she did not expect one. She had risen, and when Angus had opened the door for her, she looked up at him and spoke with obvious sincerity.

'It's so nice to have someone like yourself in charge of us. That's what makes these *Empresses* so comfortable. The last time I travelled on an ordinary coach, we were shepherded about by a dreadful man who addressed us through a megaphone. I said to him at last "My good man, I am not a film star." '

She seemed to think this a good exit line. Angus thought so too. Smiling to himself, he gathered his papers together and prepared for the formalities of the crossing.

The sea, he saw presently, was blue, and so mirror-smooth that it seemed to be another proof of Sir Claud's excellent planning. Across the water was France, and in France the journey would really begin. Angus felt his spirits rising.

The crossing was uneventful and the presence of Lord Lorrimer, or the reputation of the *Green Empresses*, sent them through the customs with a speed and ease amounting almost to diplomatic immunity. No sooner had they touched French soil than it seemed they were rolling onward, on towards the South, where some of France's loveliest scenery awaited them.

France, Spain, Portugal. Angus, putting away his papers, allowed his mind to leap ahead through the successive stages of the journey. None of it would be new to him; all of it would be full of memories. He was to see it all again – and this time, he wouldn't be paying to see it; he was actually being paid.

He was confident that he could perform his duties well. Everything, he felt, was in hand. The success of the trip was assured. Nothing could go wrong.

And for twenty-four hours, nothing did.

CHAPTER 2

THEY stopped for lunch at a small village not far from Calais. On their arrival at the Inn, Ferdy was kept busy carrying suitcases out of the coach, for the air of France seemed to have made the passengers clothes-conscious, and there was a general desire to change into holiday wear.

The men were soon ready; they sat waiting for the women on the terrace outside the Inn, and the landlord brought out small tables and placed them in the sun. When at last the women appeared, their entry was in the nature of a dress parade: Angela and Miss Seton first, in pretty, light woollen dresses; Mrs Denby-Warre in a severe suit of dark grey, and last of all, Mrs Zoller, dazzling in a close-fitting skirt and a peasant-style blouse worn perilously low on the shoulders.

There was no noticeable enthusiasm when, after a discourse on the specialities of Picardy, the landlord offered them a *pot au feu* made of frogs' legs. They chose, instead, partridges roasted in butter, with a sauce of apples and partridge livers.

Waiting for the food, they fell into groups, chatting or sitting silent or dozing. Mrs Denby-Warre came across to talk to Angus, and presently they were joined by Mrs Zoller, who had little to say at first, being occupied in staring with her usual frankness at the dresses of the other women. Having given Mrs Denby-Warre a long look, she put a question.

26

'You do not,' she asked her, 'feel yourself too warm in those winter clothes?'

'This suit,' Mrs Denby-Warre informed her coldly, 'is not winter weight.'

'It looks so hot, and the cut . . . You have a good figure, slim, straight; you should show it. Even for your age, that suit is too old. Why are you not drinking something?'

'I never take anything alcoholic, thank you.'

'That is a pity. It would do you good.' She looked at the other woman's stout, sensible shoes. 'Where do you buy your shoes?'

'I – ' Mrs Denby-Warre hesitated and looked appealingly at Angus.

'You should go always to Florence to buy your shoes,' said Mrs Zoller. 'You have good feet, so you should wear good shoes. Have you somewhere to write the address? And if you wish to buy eau de cologne, I know a shop in Madrid . . . '

Mesmerised, Mrs Denby-Warre found herself bringing out a battered little address book and borrowing a pencil from Angus. Handing it to her, he supposed that she could not bring herself to scratch out the eyes of a woman who used them to discover that she had good feet and a good figure.

He was relieved when lunch was announced. Maurice Tarrant and Mr Holt came to join him at his table, and he spent the meal listening to their comments on the other passengers. Mr Holt said little, Maurice a little too much, and at last the other man leaned back in his chair and looked at him wonderingly.

'Boy, you sure like talking,' he commented. 'But you'd better stop talking about the customers; you're making Angus here feel uncomfortable.'

'That's just his habit of discretion,' explained Maurice. 'Keeping his mouth shut in the Silent Service tradition. Did you know he'd been in the Navy?'

'In the Navy, huh?' Mr Holt turned an interested gaze on Angus. 'Why'd you get out?'

'He was invalided out,' said Maurice.

'Illness?' asked Mr Holt sympathetically.

'Rugger accident,' said Angus. 'Knee went.'

He saw that Lord Lorrimer had risen; soon they were all seated out on the terrace, drowsy with good food and wine, watching their coffee as it dripped slowly from tin containers into small, thick white cups.

Back once more in his own compartment, Angus told himself that he was fortunate to have got the job. It was unbelievably pleasant – and it was easy. Or it would be easy if Angela Clunes behaved all the way as she had behaved at lunch, making no move to join him or to talk to him. That way, he could be at peace, he thought. If there was mockery in her eyes when they met his, he could ignore it; she had caught him off guard once and it wouldn't do to give her a second chance.

He looked out of his window. They were passing sleepy Norman villages; the fields were green and grey and pale gold. Timbered cottages with thatched roofs flashed by and then there was a glimpse of a faded-looking manor set in a wild garden, or a château half hidden among trees. The coach followed the bend of a river, and Angus saw quiet reflections mirrored in the water.

Soon the Admiral came in to speak to him. He left the door open and, from the coach, a hum of conversation sounded. The talk appeared to have become general.

'How far do we get tonight?' enquired the Admiral.

'Just beyond Rouen, sir,' Angus told him.

'Do we stay one night, or two?' asked Mr Holt.

'One. We stay two nights at Beynac.'

'Daresay there'll be more to see when we get farther south,' said the Admiral, with a disparaging glance out of the window.

'And more to drink,' said Maurice Tarrant. 'Funny thing, isn't it, how these Normans don't make any wine?'

'They make Camembert and they make Calvados; that's fame enough,' said Mr Holt.

Angus was called over to adjust Mrs Zoller's window-blind. He adjusted a head cushion to prevent Mr Zoller's head from hitting the window as he slept, and then returned to his compartment to find Miss Seton installed in the observation chair.

'How are you enjoying the work?' she asked, as he sat beside her.

If every passenger were like her, he thought, the work would be even more pleasant than it was. Studying her at leisure, he found that his first estimate of her had done less than justice to her charm. Completely unassuming, completely natural, she had a repose of manner that he seldom found in women. Apart from her remarkable eyes, she had no claim to beauty; her nose was small and even snub; her mouth was large and her skin on the sallow side, but he felt that her eyes, her beautiful voice and her charm of manner gave her the right to compete with most of her better-endowed sisters.

'I like the job very much,' he said, in answer to her question. 'Are you enjoying the trip?'

'I shall enjoy it when it really begins. That'll be somewhere in the region of the Loire. But' – she turned to smile at him – 'I didn't come in here to talk about the scenery. I came about something else – something personal. In the coach just now, I heard the Admiral talking to his sister about you, and what he said interested me.'

'He gave me a good character?'

'It wasn't your character I was interested in – it was the brief history he was giving her. I couldn't help overhearing, and I began to wonder if you were once a young sub-lieutenant who, with a number of other sub-lieutenants, used to stay at a house called Haley Lodge, in Dorset.'

He was unable, for some moments, to answer. He could only stare at her as memories rushed back, crowding into his mind and driving out the present. He was back . . . back once more to a happy summer during which life had been unequally divided between brief duties at sea and prolonged pleasures on land. Haley . . . and the gang . . .

He saw Miss Seton's solicitous glance upon him.

'I said something?' she asked anxiously.

'No. That is, yes. My mind swung off for a moment – back to Haley and the beautiful, beautiful Rosamond Blake. Did you know her?'

'She's my sister.' She corrected herself. 'My half-sister.'

'Your . . . but I don't remember meeting you down at Haley?'

'I was very seldom there. I'm almost ten years older than Rosamond, and in the days when you and all those other handsome young men were wasting time down in the country, I was working in London. I went home for weekends sometimes, but only when I was certain that the house wasn't going to be full of Rosamond's young men.'

'That was a summer,' he said slowly. 'When I see her on the screen nowadays, I think that, lovely as she is, she isn't as lovely as she was when we all used to go swimming in that pool near the house. None of us thought, then, that she'd become a world name within the next few years. Tell me about her.'

'Don't you read enough about her?'

29

'I meant the other things – the things the papers don't know. Has she changed?'

'If you mean has she become spoilt – no. She's changed, of course; people do change and go on changing. But the nicest change, for me, was the fact that we've grown much closer in the last year or so. Perhaps that wasn't so much a change in her as the fact that the gap between our ages began to close. A little starlet of twenty-one or two didn't have much in common with a thirty-two-year-old sister working in London. But a woman of twenty-eight, as she is now . . . She has to be away a good deal, of course, but whenever she's home, she lives with my mother and myself at the flat. It's the one address reporters don't know.'

'Your mother' – Angus gave a reminiscent grin – 'must have got pretty tired of us in the old days.'

'She adored you all. When you get back to London, you must come and see us.'

'I'd love to. Give my love to Rosamond when you write.'

'I'll do better than that; I'll give it to her in person. I'm on my way to see her.'

'*See* her? Is she in Portugal?'

'At this moment, she's on a ship on her way to South America, but it calls at several places in Europe first, and Lisbon's one of them. When I discovered this from the shipping company, I couldn't resist the chance of seeing her. I needed a holiday, and so I decided to give her a surprise and meet her at Lisbon. I shall only see her for a few hours, but it'll be worth it.'

'She doesn't know you're coming?'

'No. My mother and I had hoped she'd come home for a short while – she's just finished a film in Italy – but she wrote to tell us she'd been made a wonderfully tempting offer; somebody bought a play – bought the playwright too, I think – and is offering her an enormous sum to appear in the film. So she said she would. That meant that we wouldn't see her for months, and so I decided I'd go to Lisbon. I had a difficult time getting a seat on this coach; the one they offered me would have got there too late. But I had a friend who – '

' – who said you were Rosamond Blake's sister?'

'No. Nobody knows that, thank goodness. My mother and I like to live in what's called happy anonymity. People know that Rosamond's real name is Blake, but even if they know she has a sister called Seton, there are so many Setons. But I'd rather you didn't mention the connection to anyone.'

'Of course I won't. How did you get on the coach in the end?'

'Lady Tarrant got me on.'

'Any relation to our wild young man?'

'Mother. I don't know her personally, but I meet her sometimes on business – she has connections with the firm I work for. She's a distant relation of Sir Claud's, and she said she'd use her influence if I'd promise to keep an eye on her son and see that he got to Lisbon. I said I would – but I hadn't seen him then.'

'Why wouldn't he want to get to Lisbon?'

'He's going to see about a job there. She thinks he'll – '

' – get cold feet before he gets there?'

'Yes. He's not a *bad* character, you know. I talked to him before lunch, and quite liked him.'

Angus lapsed into dreams. Rosamond Blake . . .

'Angela Clunes reminds me a little of Rosamond,' said Miss Seton after a time. 'She's younger, of course; she can't be more than twenty-four – but she has the same colouring, and she's got the same . . . the same *aliveness*. Comparatively few people, I find, are really alive, but Angela Clunes is one of them. Do you like Mr Yule?'

'I know nothing about Mr Yule, I'm afraid.'

'Very discreet and highly commendable. But I don't care for him, and I hope you'll do your best to prevent him from monopolising Angela Clunes. After all, there are two other young men on the coach.'

'Wouldn't Mr Holt like to hear you make that three?'

'I don't think so. Mr Holt has shown a proper sense of values by recognising my more mature charms. I don't think Angela Clunes will take Maurice seriously, and I hope she won't encourage Mr Yule.'

'Why not?' Angus could not help asking. 'He's extremely eligible.'

She hesitated.

'There's something about him,' she said at last, 'that I don't trust. So don't' – she gave him an odd, attractive little grin – 'don't get too professional, will you?'

'Too – ?'

'I mean, let Angela Clunes be friendly if she wants to be friendly.'

'Wouldn't it be safer to remain entirely professional?'

'For her, no. As I said, I don't trust Lionel Yule. I – '

She paused. The door had opened and Mr Holt had joined them.

'He's fine and big and handsome,' he told Miss Seton, 'but doesn't he belong to us all?'

'Come and take this seat,' she offered. 'I'm going inside.'

'No, no, no. You stay right where you are,' he said. 'I just came in to ask Angus about this place we're staying at tonight.'

'It's a place just outside a village called Léry,' said Angus. 'The scenery isn't spectacular, but the house is old and, I'm told, interesting.'

He had nothing further to answer for some time, for Miss Seton and Mr Holt seemed content to stay in the compartment, saying little, but displaying a quiet companionship that made Angus feel they were a well-matched pair. From the coach came a continuous hum of conversation, through which Mr Zoller slept on undisturbed.

Angus's first duty, on arriving at the stopping place, was to telephone to London and report their arrival. This done, he went to the office to check the night's arrangements. The hotel, like all the *Green Empress* hotels, was in charge of a local manager, and as the stout, smiling figure rose to greet him, Angus registered another mark of Sir Claud's attention to detail, for Monsieur Chabrun, with his plump, red cheeks, small black moustache, round stomach and pointed little feet was almost too typical, almost too picturesque.

Angus checked the rooms and collected the mail. There was not much: two telegrams for Lord Lorrimer, a postcard for Angela, a letter or two for the others. Angus distributed them, keeping Angela's until the last.

'Thank you,' she said, as he handed her the card. 'Isn't this a wonderful old place? There's a four-poster in my bedroom.'

'In all the bedrooms. It's a nice touch.'

'I'm certain they've got perfectly good electricity which they switch off just as we drive up – and then they get the candles out. It's almost overdoing it, but candlelight's very becoming. Is anybody at your table for dinner tonight, or can I join you?'

He told her that he would be delighted, and went to his room to have a bath and change. Going down later to the long, low dining-room, his pleasure on seeing her was considerably lessened by seeing that Lionel Yule was also to make one of the party.

At dinner, he did his best to keep the conversation flowing, but it was not easy. Angela was thoughtful, and Yule sulky; Angus suspected that he, too, had hoped there would be no third.

'You're tired?' he suggested to Angela at last.

'Not tired, no. I'm depressed.'

'If there's anything about the *Green Empress* you don't like, I'll send a cable to headquarters and have it altered instantly.'

She smiled, but with none of her early gaiety.

'I used the wrong adjective. I'm not depressed, I'm worried. And Lionel's worried, too – aren't you, Lionel?'

Mr Yule, after some thought, admitted that his mind was not entirely at rest.

'I'm worried about my father.' Her tone was dejected.

Angus sent a glance in Lord Lorrimer's direction.

'He seems more cheerful than he was this morning,' he said.

'He's got something on his mind, and it's something serious, or it wouldn't be having this effect on him. If it were something to do with work, Lionel would know what it was. If it was a – a sort of domestic worry, then I'd know about it. But neither Lionel nor I can think of anything.'

'Why don't you ask your father what it is?' suggested Angus.

'I did. He said he was trying to work something out, and felt rather tired.'

'He's more than tired,' said Lionel. 'He's . . . I've never seen him like this before.'

And you, thought Angus with a savagery that surprised himself, ought to be damn well reassuring her instead of sitting there droning out more misery.

Prejudice, he told himself, must be a potent thing, for Miss Seton's opinion of Yule seemed to have altered his own. He had summed him up as the typical private secretary: sauve, competent, his personality tailored to the job, a glossy smoothness overlying his natural manner. He had held aloof from the rest of the passengers, devoting a good deal of time to the papers in the despatch case, working on them with a touch of ostentation that had more than once called forth a sarcastic remark from Maurice Tarrant. Angus had admitted to himself that there had been some grounds for Tarrant's irritation; Yule had the air of doing work that nobody could do as well as himself – but until now, he had not actively disliked him. He could only put his aversion down to the fact that Miss Seton, on whose judgement and intelligence he was prepared to rely, had said that she disliked and distrusted the man.

He made up his mind that he would not care how little he saw of Mr Yule during the next few days . . . or how much of Angela Clunes. Lively or depressed, he found her filling more and more of his mind.

When dinner was over, he went to see how Ferdy was faring. He found him in the large, stone-floored kitchen, seated at the remains of his meal. Drawing out a chair, Angus sat down opposite and studied the fat, flushed face.

'How?' he enquired.

'This is the part I like, sir,' said Ferdy. 'This is the fleshpots. I enjoy a hard day's driving, but when I'm at the wheel, I'm better empty. I don't do more than pick at lunch, and as for this wine they dish out so freely . . . no, sir. But when we've got where we're going, when I've seen to the *Empress* and got her safely bedded down and locked away, then I can let m'self go.' He counted the empty dishes arrayed before him. 'I dunno what I've eaten, sir, but it was all nice'n oiyl, and it all slipped down a treat. How's things with you, sir?'

'Going well, I think.'

'No hitches?'

'His lordship seems a bit out of spirits, but that's all.'

'I'd noticed that,' said Ferdy reflectively. 'I've driven him before, and he was always one of the party, so to speak. What's on his mind, sir?'

'His daughter doesn't know and his secretary doesn't know.'

'He's probably done in,' said Ferdy sagely. 'What they call the price of office . . . or something.' He stretched. 'Well, sir, I'm going to bed m'self down near the *Empress* before this dinner begins to take effect.'

Angus looked at him curiously.

'Is it really necessary for the drivers – '

' – to stay close to the *Empresses*?' Ferdy's broad face broadened still further in a smile. 'I don't know how necessary it is, sir, but I know there isn't one of us drivers who'd leave the *Empress* alone day or night.'

'What could happen?'

'Oh . . . nothing, probably, sir. But they're expensive buses and they've got expensive parts and expensive fittings. You'd be surprised how many people just like to take a look-see. But

34

I've got her tuned up and I know that if nobody else puts a finger on her, she'll run for ten thousand miles without a mite of trouble. And so . . . nobody else is going to put a finger on her.'

'Sound enough.' Angus rose. 'Good night, Ferdy.'

'Good night, sir. Eleven o'clock start tomorrow?'

'Yes.'

Angus went to his room. Having undressed, he climbed with some misgiving into the four-poster and settled himself between the sheets, and then got up again to draw back the curtains so that when he opened his eyes in the morning, the view would be before him.

But when his eyes opened, it was still dark. He lay for some moments shaking off the mists of sleep, and knew even during that short time that something or someone had wakened him. Sitting up with a jerk, he saw the flicker of a candle and heard a whisper in French.

'Monsieur, are you awake?'

'Yes. Is that Monsieur Chabrun?'

'Yes, Monsieur.'

'What is it?'

'It is the telephone, Monsieur. Somebody wishes to speak to Mademoiselle Seton. The person is waiting.'

Angus sat still. He could now make out the stout form of the manager; he could see a long nightshirt and below it, slippered feet, but he took in the details without registering them, for his mind was considering the alternatives of speaking to the caller himself, or waking Miss Seton.

He peered at his watch. There was nothing in his orders about waking a passenger at two in the morning to answer the telephone. On the other hand, nobody in their senses would ring at this time unless the message was of the first importance.

He decided that he must wake her. He rose and consulted his room plan, not because he did not know it already, but because he must make absolutely certain that he did not disturb the wrong person.

'I will wake Mademoiselle Seton,' he told Monsieur Chabrun. 'Please say that she is coming at once.'

He put on a dressing gown, lit his candle and made his way down two short, winding flights of stairs to Miss Seton's room, deciding as he went that candles and oak beams and four-posters were all very well as atmosphere, but not to be compared with up-to-date comforts – and telephones in every bedroom.

He reached Miss Seton's door and knocked once, twice, softly. There was no reply. He opened the door, took a few steps into the room and spoke her name in a low tone.

'Miss Seton.'

There was an instant's pause, and then a stirring behind the curtains of the huge bed. Then she had sat upright and had spoken his name.

'It's Mr Graham. What is it?'

'I'm sorry to disturb you, but you're wanted on the telephone. It must be important, I think – it's five past two, and nobody – '

But she was out of bed; he heard the rasp of silk as she put on a dressing gown. She reached for a comb, drew it through her hair and went quietly to the door.

'Take the candle,' said Angus in a low voice. 'I'll go ahead and show you where the phone is.'

She followed him downstairs; the only sound was the creak-creak of the old stairs. He led her to the little room in which Monsieur Chabrun stood carefully holding the receiver, as though putting it down would break the connection. He handed it to her and followed Angus out of the room and closed the door.

'I hope,' he whispered to Angus, 'that it will not be bad news.'

'I hope so too. Please go back to bed, Monsieur. I will stay here and see that Miss Seton is all right.'

He heard the creaking of the stairs, and stood alone in the great hall. He could hear at intervals the murmur of Miss Seton's voice, but the intervals were long; she was doing more listening than talking. Once, he thought he heard a sharp exclamation, but he could not be sure. Then there was the sound of the receiver being replaced, and he waited for her to join him.

But the minutes passed, and she did not come out of the room. Angus wondered whether he had been mistaken; perhaps she was still on the line. But from the other room there came not a sound; no murmur, no movement.

He waited for what he felt to be an age – and then he opened the door and spoke without entering the room.

'Miss Seton?'

He could see her form silhouetted against the long window.

She was standing quite still, so still that a chill went through him.

'Are you all right?' he asked softly.

She did not answer for some time, but he knew that she had heard. At last her voice came, and it was perfectly steady.

'Yes. I'm . . . all right.'

He went up to her and lifted the candle from the table and held it so that its light showed her face. Its pallor shocked him. He thought of her mother and her sister, and put an anxious question.

'Is your . . . is anybody ill?'

'No. No, thank you.'

'Sit down,' he said. 'I'm going to find you a drink.'

'No. No, thank you. I'll be all right.'

'There hasn't been any . . . any kind of accident?'

She shook her head.

'No. It wasn't that kind of bad news . . . '

'I'm going to find you a drink,' he said again. 'But not down here. You must go back to bed, and I'll bring one up to you.'

He led her silently up the stairs and left her in her room. Then he made his way to the dining-room. There was nothing to be found there, but in the kitchen there was wine, and with a glass in his hand, he went back to Miss Seton's room and, knocking softly, entered and closed the door. His voice and movements were hushed; Maurice Tarrant's room was on one side, Mr Holt's on the other. He hoped that they were not light sleepers.

She took the glass, drank the wine and lay back in bed.

'Thank you. That was kind of you,' she said.

'I'm sorry you've had bad news.' He gave her an anxious look. 'Is there nothing I can do?'

'You won't mention to anybody that I . . . that I was rung up?'

'Of course not.'

'Would you light my candle for me, please?'

He lit it and then, as there seemed nothing more he could do, he went back to his room and lay in the darkness wondering what she had heard and who had relayed the bad news. He knew that something had shaken her badly, and he admired the way in which she had kept her control. Would she, he wondered, leave the coach and return to England? She would scarcely be in a mood to continue the journey.

Dawn was breaking before he fell asleep. When he awoke, the view was before him, and he got out of bed and looked at it – but it was an absent look. His mind was on what had happened in the early hours of the morning.

Miss Seton in trouble. Lord Lorrimer was depressed, Maurice Tarrant an unknown quantity, and Angela Clunes ...

Perhaps, he reflected, this job wasn't going to be so easy, after all.

CHAPTER 3

ACCORDING to his instructions, Angus's first duty each morning was to see the driver and assure himself that the night had passed without incident. On his way to seek out Ferdy, however, he paused at Miss Seton's door. It was still early; too early, he felt, to knock and ask how she was feeling. As he stood hesitating, the door of her room opened and a maid came out carrying a tray. In the room, already dressed, was Miss Seton. Seeing Angus, she came to the door to speak to him, and he saw that although she was pale and had heavy shadows under her eyes, her manner was perfectly calm.

'Good morning. I came along to see how you were,' he said.

'I'm a little tired, but that's all. Thank you for being so kind last night.'

'This morning,' he corrected. 'Why didn't you have a long rest in bed? We're not starting until eleven.'

'I wanted to get out of doors. I feel better outside – and I'd like some exercise. I'll go for a walk, but I'll be back in time to pack.'

'Sure there's nothing I can do?'

'Nothing, thank you. I'm perfectly all right.'

Relieved, he went on to find Ferdy, and came upon him at last at the door of the garage. His stout form was bent forward and he seemed to be studying some object on the ground. As Angus approached, he straightened and indicated the spot at which he had been staring.

' 'Morning, sir. Care to come and look at this?'

Angus, puzzled, approached and looked down at the place, but saw nothing that could account for Ferdy's interest.

'Anything wrong?' he asked.

'Nothing, sir – but there might have been, if I hadn't been sleeping near by.'

'Prowlers?'

'I think so, sir. I heard someone trying the bolts. If you look close, you'll see footmarks on the ground.'

Angus frowned.

'What time was this?'

'About five o'clock it was, sir. Something woke me – I sleep light – and I listened for a bit, and then I heard someone having a go at the bolts. That didn't worry me; they're strong, and I didn't think it'd be long before they found out how strong, and gave up trying. But I wanted to get a look at who it was, and so I nipped out of bed and waited by the window, thinking I'd see 'em as they went by. But I picked the wrong window; he hopped off the long way round; I didn't get a look at him – or them.' Longing came into his voice. 'If we were staying one more night, sir, I'd wait up and take a swipe.' He gave Angus a belligerent glare, squared his shoulders and thumped a chest as hard as iron. 'I've been in some scraps in m'time, sir, and a driver-mechanic's job isn't as soft as people think. I'm in good fighting trim and I'd hand out more than I took.'

'Why didn't you come and call me?'

Ferdy was obviously on the point of stating that he could take on all comers without aid, but there was no time to say so; the Admiral, with Angela by his side, had strolled into view and stopped beside them.

'Good morning,' said Angela. 'We're looking for breakfast.'

Angus's eyes rested on her. The morning was sunny, but cold, and she was wearing a light woollen coat in a shade of pale yellow that he had hitherto believed unbecoming to a blonde. He saw that he had been mistaken. Against the colours of the garden – the pale and tender green of spring, the deeper green of pine, the purple of lilac – she made a picture he did not think he would easily forget.

The Admiral's booming voice recalled him.

'Came down to try to get something to eat,' he said.

'Wasn't breakfast taken up to your room, sir?' asked Angus.

'If you call it breakfast. When you said breakfast last night, I thought you meant breakfast, but all they brought up was a gill of coffee and a couple of those crescent-shaped pastry affairs and a thimbleful of apricot jam.' He shuddered. 'Might do for a woman.'

'It didn't do for me,' said Angela. 'I polished it off and came down to get something solid to eat.'

Angus led them to the dining-room, where they found Mr Holt at a long table, eating the hearty breakfast he had ordered the night before. The cloud passing from his face, the Admiral took his place between Angela and Angus, opened his large, starched table napkin and spread it on his knees. When Angus had twice bent to pick it up from the floor, the old man tucked it under his chin and bent to do justice to a good meal. Angus, watching Angela, found himself correcting another theory: that women merely pecked at some toast in the morning. She ate almost as much as the Admiral, and in half the time.

There was not, at first, much conversation. After a time the Admiral, pouring himself out his third cup of coffee, referred to the scene he had witnessed earlier.

'When we came up to you,' he said to Angus, 'I thought that driver fellow looked angry. Any hanky-panky during the night?'

'None, sir,' Angus assured him. 'Somebody tried the garage bolts, that's all.'

'And didn't get in, eh?'

'No. I gather from the driver that there's often a certain amount of local curiosity concerning the *Empresses*.'

'Well, there's a lot of stuff in them that I expect some people would like to get their hands on,' said the Admiral. 'They're expensively fitted out. The tyres are worth a packet, and I daresay a few of those engine parts would come in handy. Did the driver get a look at the chap?'

'Unfortunately not.'

'Fortunately not,' corrected Mr Holt. 'I bet he can use his fists.'

'So can you, can't you?' said the Admiral to Angus. 'Didn't I hand you a trophy some years ago, at Dartmouth?'

'You did, sir. It wasn't strictly deserved; my last two opponents went down with mumps.'

'I remembered you.' There was no compliment in the words except to the Admiral's powers of memory. 'Placed you at once. I'm sorry you're out of the Service. How long is it now?'

'Two years, sir.'

'What've you been doing since?' asked Mr Holt.

'Looking for a job, mostly.'

The Admiral looked shocked.

'What? Young fella like you, with a Naval training behind him – '

'There were office jobs,' explained Angus, 'but I suppose it was the Naval training that made them seem rather cramping. If you start in an office, you can go on in one, but after nearly nine years in the Navy, I wanted to get something with a bit of moving about, if I could.'

'And did you?' the Admiral wanted to know.

'I think so. This oil job seems to involve a certain amount of work away from a desk.'

'Good pay?' enquired Mr Holt, with a friendly interest that made Angus smile.

'Eventually, I hope.'

The door opened, and Maurice Tarrant came into the room and stood looking at them. Early as it was, he seemed to be in his usual high spirits.

'Why didn't I get invited to this party?' he demanded.

'I heard you ordering your breakfast last night,' Angela told him. 'You asked for a huge one.'

'That's what's wrong with these old buildings,' complained Maurice. 'Sounds carry. Take last night – or rather, take the early hours of this morning. Creak, creak, creak on the stairs, and cautious knocks on doors and candles flickering on landings.' He clicked his tongue reproachfully. 'People ought to be more discreet.'

'Who,' asked the Admiral, 'was walking about the house?'

'If Angus knew, he wouldn't tell us,' said Maurice. 'And that,' he added coolly, 'is why I took the trouble to get up to look.'

Angus stared at him, a frown gathering on his brow.

'You – '

'Now, now, now,' said Maurice soothingly. 'Don't get cross. I wanted to satisfy my curiosity, that's all. I know that boys will be boys, but I had to find out who the girls were.'

'And if you found out,' said Angela, 'I hope you'll have the decency to keep it to yourself.'

'Cross my heart,' said Maurice.

The Admiral rose.

'Any objection to my going along to talk to the driver?' he asked Angus. 'I'd like to hear exactly what happened.'

Angus had no objection to make, and Maurice looked after the Admiral thoughtfully as he went out.

'What's he going to see the driver for?' he enquired.

'Somebody tried the garage bolts last night,' said Mr Holt.

'No – really?' said Maurice. 'I must look into this.'

He followed the Admiral out of the room, and Mr Holt stood hesitating for a moment. Then he gave a slightly malicious smile.

'You two won't mind,' he asked, 'if I go with them and leave you alone?'

'We won't mind at all,' said Angela. 'But if we're going to be alone, we'll go out of doors. Come on, Angus.'

The three went out of the room. Mr Holt walked in the direction of the garage, and Angela led Angus towards the road.

'Is there time for a walk?' she asked.

'A short one.'

'Then let's go through the village. I like looking at all the little shops.'

He walked beside her, wondering, as they went, what had become of Lionel Yule. She answered the unspoken question.

'My father's working, and Lionel's with him. A bit hard to have to work on the journey – but then you're working too,' she remembered. 'Are you enjoying it?'

'Yes. Are you?'

'Of course. Were you angry with Maurice just now?'

'I thought he was talking a little too much.'

'Yes . . . but I don't think he always knows what he's talking about.'

'I think he does.'

She threw him a glance.

'You don't like him?'

He hesitated, and saw her quick frown. She stopped and faced him, and the owner of the *charcuterie* outside which they had halted prepared to receive them, but they did not notice him.

'You can't talk to me about the passengers, because you're a courier – is that it?' she demanded.

'Something like that.'

'For goodness sake,' she said slowly, 'can't you get off your high horse?'

He frowned.

'I'm on one?'

'Of course. You're trying to be the perfect courier, and you're overdoing it, just as you overdid the no-more-Navy decision. Why? You're simply doing this job to fill in time, so why not relax and have fun – with me?'

'I'm being paid to look after the passengers,' he pointed

out, 'not to amuse myself with the prettiest girl aboard. Besides . . . '

Once more, he paused. She turned and walked slowly on, and he fell into step beside her. When they had walked in silence for some time, she glanced up at him.

'I'm still waiting,' she said.

'For what?'

'For the end of the sentence. I know what the end of it is, but if I don't make you say it yourself, you'll remain as you are: stiff and stand-offish, and we shall never get any further.'

'And that,' said Angus deliberately, 'might be a very good thing.'

She took his hand and turned him round to face her. A small boy carrying loaves a yard long paused to study them. Two women with baskets on their arms came to a standstill and gave them curious glances. The baker stared from his doorway, but Angus and Angela were conscious only of one another.

'Why would it be a good thing?' she asked. 'It would be a bad thing to like me and be afraid to say so.' She gave his arm an angry shake. 'You've got to get out of this mood, Angus. You've got to pull yourself out of this My-whole-life-was-the-Navy-and-now-my-life-is-ended mood. You've got to – *got* to throw off this fit of the sulks.' She saw his face whiten, and went swiftly on: 'Because that's all it is, dearest Angus, and you've got to – *got* to see it. It was hellishly bad luck, but it happens to other people all the time, and they have to put it behind them and just go on without dragging it behind them all the time – as you're doing.'

'I – '

'Wait, please! Everybody knows it. All your old friends know it. Oliver knows it. I know it. Your friends have tried to pull you out of it, but you wouldn't be pulled. You've avoided them, and you've avoided Oliver. And now I've caught up with you, and I'm not going to sit for the next week or more watching you avoiding me. Unless, of course, you loathe me and don't want to see me. Do you? Do you loathe me, I mean?'

He stared at her, all the misery of the past two years in his face.

'Do you?' she persisted. 'Do let's have this out, Angus; it may be our only chance for the whole of the trip. Do you like me at all? Please . . . *please* tell me!'

'You . . . you represent, for me,' he said, speaking with difficulty, 'everything I want in the world. You – or do I mean somebody like you? No; you. You, and all you mean: somebody I could have grown up with; somebody who knew me and the men round me; somebody who talks my language, who knows the people and the things I never thought I'd have to give up. I didn't sulk. I tried – God knows how hard – to make a new life on the fringe of the old one. Everybody was kind. Everyone knew someone who knew someone who was going to give me a job – the kind of job I wanted. And that's all it ever came to. People wanted to help, but everything . . . came to nothing. The months went by and I was still out of a job and people were still promising to find me one. I got one or two on my own, but they led nowhere except to a life spent at a desk in a city. So I looked further – and that's the whole story.'

'Not the whole story. Why do you leave out all the things that make a story interesting? Why leave out me, for instance? Would you believe me if I told you that I'd adored you from the moment I saw you?'

He smiled, his eyes warm with gratitude.

'You're sweet, but . . . no. No, I wouldn't.'

'It's true. It's true, Angus. Ask my brother. Ask my father. It's true. You were . . . if you laugh, I'll kill you . . . you represented my ideal man. You were tall and strong and breathtakingly handsome, and I couldn't, I just couldn't believe that we wouldn't get together – one day. But you didn't even notice me! Oliver knew how I felt, but he would have died before he'd have done anything to help me to get hold of you. He thought you were much, much too good for me. And I waited, feeling certain that I'd catch up with you in time. But . . . you left the Navy, and we lost you. Oliver tried to keep in touch with you, but you made it very difficult for him. But I was still sure – I still had a feeling we'd meet. And then . . . I got on the coach, and there you were.' She paused. 'I suppose you think I shouldn't be telling you this?'

'Perhaps you shouldn't – but it's good hearing.' He smiled. 'Are you always so impulsive?'

'Impulsive?' She considered. 'No. No, I'm not impulsive at all. I might rush at things, but only when I've made quite certain that I want them. And I only rush if rushing's necessary. Don't forget that we really know one another quite well, even if we haven't often met.'

44

'You can't really know very much about me,' he pointed out gently.

She laughed, and he liked the sound.

'No? I know everything about you – up to the time you left the Navy. I know what you've done, where you've been, even what you've said. I know all the times you've kept Oliver out of trouble. I know the name of every girl you took out; he used to make a point of telling me. Oh yes . . . I know a great deal about you, and that gives me rather an advantage, since you know a good deal less about me – beyond the fact that I appear over-impulsive. All you need to know about me is that I've got a quick temper. Quick, but not bad. And I'm said to have a lot of sense, and if only I can make you see sense now, we can . . . Oh, Angus,' she begged, 'please don't make things too difficult! Try to see this straight. I get on to the coach and . . . there you are, I get my breath back and then I go and talk to you, and don't find you very friendly. I wait to see if you'll pick it up where I left off – and at lunch, you ignore me. I saw that you'd made up your mind that you were going to keep it absolutely official – courier to passenger. Last night at dinner, I wasn't only depressed about my father. I was feeling that it was going to be murder just to sit in the coach seeing you all the time, all the way to Lisbon, and . . . and never getting anywhere. I know you've never looked seriously at a girl, because Oliver said so. You wouldn't look while you were in the Navy, and later, you took that old, dead stand about having nothing to offer a woman et cetera et cetera. And you're still taking it. You've got *everything* to offer a woman: good health, a splendid body, a fine mind and a clean one, a decent record, a good background . . . yourself. If you want to take it all to Canada and waste it on some ghastly girl you hardly know, then do; I can't stop you. All I can do is try. All I want you to do is remember that I've waited for years hoping that fate would throw us together – and it has. And this is the last chance I'll ever have, and I'm going to take it. I have taken it. Are you going to sit and be a beastly courier from now on, or are we going to be friends and try to make up for all the time we've lost? Quick: Yes or no?'

He stared down at her.

'Do you . . . do you know what you're saying?'

Once more she laughed, and in the sound was happiness, and utter trust, and love. He tried to speak, and found that his throat had become too restricted for speech. He took her hand

45

and held it, and she waited, but no words came from him. Then, to the ecstasy of the onlookers, now swelled to a small crowd, he put his arms round her and bent and laid his lips on hers. He kept them there for some time; he had intended to put into the kiss the flood of gratitude that filled him, but when their lips touched, he found his clinging. Gratitude melted in the warmth and scent of her mouth. When at last he raised his head, it was not gratitude that he felt.

'Angus . . . '

'You're so sweet,' he murmured. 'You're so sweet. You're as angelic as your name, and as gentle, and as kind. But – '

'You needn't go on.'

'Hadn't we' – he smiled; a smile with so much love in it that her heart turned over – 'had we better face facts?'

'We've just faced them. We're made for one another and it would be madness not to get together. We've known one another for years and years, and so we needn't dally with the preliminaries.'

'There are certain things that . . . ' He paused and looked round, taking in the size and sentiments of the audience. 'I suppose,' he said slowly, 'we've given them a wonderful show?'

He took her hand and led her firmly away.

'Where are you taking me to?'

'Away from the local inhabitants. I want to talk to you.'

He said nothing until they were beyond the village, walking down a quiet, leafy lane by a stream. He found a grassy bank and settled her on it and sat by her side.

'Now,' he said, 'we'll talk common sense. Are you listening?'

She did not appear to be listening. She had picked several blades of grass and held them bunched in her fist, while with the other hand she drew them out one by one and released them in the wind.

'He loves me, he loves me not,' she murmured. 'He didn't; he did, when he kissed me just now. He wouldn't; he would, having found that he wasn't dead, after all. He will; he won't ever dare to look at me again and say that I mean nothing to him. He – '

She was in his arms, and the common sense he meant to bring to bear upon the situation seemed long in making its way to the surface. But at last he released her, and they looked at one another and laughed – a long, ringing sound in which

46

could be heard her relief and happiness, his helplessness and surrender.

'You're quite hopeless,' he told her at last. 'How does one knock sense into a woman like you?'

'Common sense? You were going to talk some. Talk some.'

He turned to face her.

'Do you know how much money I've got?'

'You've got a job, haven't you?'

'A try-out job, at a salary that sounds high in England and goes nowhere on the other side of the Atlantic. In a country I don't know the first thing about.'

'And don't want to go to. Then why go?'

'Because I can't brush opportunity aside merely because I happen to love Europe and because I've enjoyed studying its history and languages. It was a nice hobby, but I can't indulge it any more. Canada – everybody knows it – is the land of opportunity, the land of the future, the land for the young and strong. If I don't want to go out there, there's something wrong with me.'

'Why? A lot of us want to stay where we belong – and you were reared under the oak and not under the maple.'

'I'm a Scot and I was –'

'Don't split hairs. What's wrong with wanting to stay where you belong?'

'The fact that I can probably make a better living in Canada. But I'm not sure how well I can do the job, and so my assets are –'

'There you go again. Angus darling, that's all so *dead*! In the old days, people used to think along those lines; everything had to be solid, and you didn't take a single step towards matrimony unless you could give your bride all that she'd been wringing out of her father for the past few years. That's dead; that's finished. All that couples set out with now is what they've screwed out of their friends in wedding presents, and some furniture they've bought on the never-never. They put their sons' names down for Eton and Harrow knowing perfectly well that their only hope of ever paying the fees will be by winning a football pool. If you can't bring home enough to clothe me, I'll take a part-time or even a full-time job, like thousands of other wives. That's common sense. Is that what you were going to say?'

'Don't you think a man likes to have something to offer?'

'No. Not any more. Because while he's amassing it, the

47

girl's lost all her bloom and is sick and tired of hanging about and losing all the best years. There's nothing irresponsible in marrying without capital. Things have moved since those cosy old days. Our grandparents educated their children out of income; our parents educated us out of a rapidly-dwindling capital; we shall educate our children by taking out educational policies when they're born and cashing them when they're in their teens. See?'

'Look – '

'Kiss me, please.'

'You think that when I kiss you, I lose my grip on facts?'

'I don't think. I'm absolutely certain. Kiss me and prove it.'

He proved it.

He did not know how he got back to the hotel. Angela's hand was in his; he could not remember whether they spoke or not. She left him at the entrance and he walked round the garden, then round again, and again, without knowing where he was going. He passed two men who looked like the Admiral and Mr Holt. On a bench in the shade was a woman who looked like Miss . . . Miss . . . yes, Seton; she was writing letters and he felt a stir of admiration for her courage – courage over what?

The passengers filed into their places; he could remember nothing about who they were, but there were no empty seats and so he presumed that everybody was present.

They were on their way and he did not, for the moment, care where they were bound. The mists would rise; the rosy clouds would disperse; when they did, he would be walking down the aisle of the coach in person and not down the aisle of a church in dreams. Soon . . . but not yet. This morning . . .

This morning he had received a gift from Heaven. He would take it – and be thankful.

CHAPTER 4

RESPONSIBILITY made itself felt as the coach journeyed southward, and Angus dragged himself reluctantly back from dreams to duty. Descending from the clouds, he took his bearings and found that the *Green Empress* was midway between Alençon and Le Mans.

Going on an inspection of the passengers, he found them still without any noticeable interest in the scenery, but on good terms with themselves and with one another. Lord Lorrimer was reading. Lionel Yule, despatch case on his knee, was studying some papers. Miss Seton's chair was still turned to face Mr Holt's; Angus, stopping for a word, found her showing less signs of tiredness. Mr Zoller was asleep; adjusting the cushions at his head, Angus went on to Mrs Zoller and found her staring intently out of the window and at intervals making notes in a little book.

'What is number seventy-eight?' she asked, as he stopped beside her.

'I think it's Seine-et-Oise, but I'll look it up for you. Are you interested in car numbers?'

'No. They are not so interesting, really,' she confessed, 'but it is something to do to pass away the time, don't you think so?'

He was saved from the necessity of replying by hearing Mr Holt address him.

'Where're we lunching, Angus?'

'At a little place called Guecelard.'

'And after that?' enquired the Admiral.

'After that, sir, we get on towards Saumur and see some nice country.'

'Saumur . . . Saumur,' mused the Admiral. 'Heard something about Saumur.'

'Why, I should say so,' said Mr Holt. 'It's – '

'Got it,' said the Admiral. 'Just come back to me. Used to be a fine Cavalry School there. Still may be, for all I know.'

'Well, I was going to mention the château,' said Mr Holt, 'but if you prefer horses, then you prefer horses.'

'Why can't you be interested in the important facts about places?' Mrs Denby-Warre asked the Admiral plaintively.

'Such as what?' he demanded.

'Well, such as . . . such as . . . '

Mr Zoller opened his eyes, fixed them hopefully on Angus, and closed them again as Angus went to prepare drinks. Lionel Yule, taking his glass of sherry, carried it into the courier's compartment and waited for Angus to join him.

'Nice view from here,' he observed, as Angus came in.

'Not bad.'

'Don't you drink on duty?'

'Not as a rule. There's a good map if you care to look at it.'

'Thanks.'

While he studied it, Angus studied him. Nothing to dislike, he reflected, but nothing much to attract anybody who didn't like conventional good looks. Well-groomed; clean sort of look about him. Not one glimmer of humour, and a slight – very slight – air of condescension. He looked the sort of fellow one would put down as completely reliable; solid, in fact. It was odd that Miss Seton had thought him untrustworthy.

Yule put aside the map and Angus realised that while he had appeared to be looking at it, he had been thinking of other matters.

'I've got something on my mind; I wonder if you can do anything about it?' he asked.

'What is it?'

'This fellow Tarrant. He's a bit of a nuisance. I think he's annoying Miss Clunes.'

'Has she said so?'

'Good Heavens, no! But one can see. I know her pretty well and – '

'Is he annoying her, or is he annoying you?'

Their eyes met, and gave nothing away.

'If he annoys anybody,' said Lionel coldly, at last, 'can't you do something about it?'

'I can only deal with facts, not with feelings. If he does anything specific, anything one can pin him down on, I can deal with it. But if it's merely his manner that irritates you, there's not much I can do.'

'There's something about him that gets under one's skin – or don't you think so?'

'He's all right. He talks a bit too much, that's all. He's irritating, but I don't think he's offensive. It's a pity he goes in for this schoolboy type of fun, but that's Tarrant and you have to take him or leave him. As he's paid his fare to Lisbon, I'm afraid we have to take him. Will you have another drink?'

'No, thank you.'

'Then I'll go and see if the others will.'

Lord Lorrimer looked up from his book as Angus paused beside him.

'I'm sorry – I hadn't realised when I first saw you that you were the Graham who was a friend of my son. You weren't at Oliver's wedding?'

'I couldn't go, unfortunately.'

'Angela tells me you're going to Canada.'

'I am, sir.'

'It's a fine country.'

One could bet, thought Angus, on exactly what people would say when they learned that a young man was going out to Canada. He had heard the inevitable observations made so often that he could now recite them from memory. He had heard them spoken by well-wishers for the past two months, and spoken with especial heartiness by those who had been unsuccessful in finding him a job in England. Canada was (a) a fine country, (b) the land of opportunity, (c) the land of the future and (d) the land for every young man of ambition.

Lord Lorrimer might have said something of the kind, but Mr Holt was speaking across the coach.

'How far to the lunch stop, Angus ? I'm hungry.'

'Me, also,' said Mrs Zoller.

They were relieved to learn that the lunch stop was not far away. Angus, making plans to get Angela to himself, found when the coach stopped that she had been making her own plans.

'You're lunching with my father – and with me, naturally,' she told him. 'Why haven't you addressed one single word to me on the coach ?'

'Guess.'

'Correct. Do you still love me ?'

'Do I have to say so ?'

'Of course. But not at the moment – here's Maurice.'

Maurice Tarrant joined them and they went in the direction of the dining-room.

'If he was just on the point of proposing to you,' he said, 'don't let me interrupt. As a matter of fact, we'd make an excellent husband for you. I could support you until my money ran out – which it's doing with regrettable speed. By that time, he'd be making some, and he could take over. He'll wear longer than I will; I'm in full possession now, but my father was as bald as a pebble at thirty, and I shall go the same way.'

'Don't you ever,' asked Angela, 'talk anything but rubbish ?'

He grinned.

'Seldom. Seldom. But when you've finished having what you think is an intelligent conversation, have you ever stopped to analyse it ? You'll find that everybody's talked tripe, but on serious topics. You can talk tripe, write tripe and act tripe – just so long as you keep it above the comedy level. I don't know why this is. I haven't had time to work it out, but you can take it as gospel. I've just proved it, as a matter of fact. I got tired of the dirty glances Mrs Denby-Warrehorse kept sending me, and so I went over and talked to her and hinted – oh, so delicately – that my manner concealed an inner tragedy. And now . . . I'm at her table for lunch, at her earnest request. So long.'

'If he could ever persuade a girl to marry him,' said Angela, looking after him thoughtfully, 'he mightn't make a bad husband. What did Lionel go and sit beside you for ? It wasn't to look at the map, was it ?'

'It was to complain about Tarrant – and it was also to tell me, in an oblique way, that he had a lien on you.'

'Well, he hasn't and he hadn't and that's that,' she said. 'Be nice to father at lunch.'

'All I want to do to your father is tell him about us.'

'Then do. It'll take his mind off his other troubles, whatever they are.'

'I'll tell him at dinner tonight.'

'Say after me: Angela Rosemary, I love you very much indeed.'

'Angela Rosemary, if you wait fifteen years, I think I'll be able to keep you in something like comfort, but in the meantime, you'll have to put up with less than the best.'

'Other women have done it.'

'Not many women have had your gilded upbringing. A man who comes asking for your hand in marriage will be expected to bring something beside his hopes. And here's your father and here's our table. Be seated, Miss Clunes.'

Lunch was a pleasant but not, today, a leisurely meal. There was a marked change in the atmosphere; a general feeling that the interesting part of the trip was about to begin. The Loire was before them; soon they would cross it on their way to the beautiful district of the Dordogne.

'It's a pity,' remarked Maurice, as they all settled themselves in the coach once more, 'that you can't put wings on cars and coaches and fly 'em over the dull bits. Especially in your country,' he told Mr Holt. 'Why don't you bring your scenic splendours closer together ?'

'We like you to build up a lot of anticipation before you get to them,' explained Mr Holt. 'Look.' He jerked his head towards the view. 'That's the Loire. Ever seen Angers, Admiral ?'

The Admiral, with an effort, roused himself.

'Who?'

'The town of Angers. Interesting place.'

'Angers? Angers? Yes, I recollect now,' said the Admiral. 'That's where they make umbrellas.'

'Well – ' began Mr Holt.

'And roofing slates,' proceeded the Admiral.

'Well, perhaps,' conceded Mr Holt. 'But it's also the home of Cointreau.'

'Who?'

'And there's a château there,' persevered Mr Holt.

'Daresay,' grunted the Admiral. 'Scores hereabouts.' He looked at Angus. 'How far do we get today?'

'To Beynac, sir.'

'Where's that?' demanded the Admiral.

'It's about sixty kilometres past Perigueux.'

'And where's that?'

'Perigord region,' said Maurice. 'Where's that? It's the district in which you eat better than anywhere else in the whole of France.'

'The home of truffles,' came unexpectedly from Mr Zoller.

'Is it true,' asked Miss Seton, 'that pigs dig up truffles?'

'It is quite true,' said Mr Zoller. 'But the pigs must be pregnant.'

Mrs Denby-Warre grew pale.

'Must be . . . ' Words failed her.

'*Enceinte*,' explained Mr Zoller kindly. 'They dig at the roots of stunted oak trees and find the truffles.'

Having given this information, he closed his eyes, and the passengers relapsed into silence. Angus closed his door and settled down for a few moments to himself, but he could see in his mirror that Maurice Tarrant had changed his seat and was in earnest conversation with Miss Seton. She looked interested in what he was saying, and Angus was glad to see that her mind was being kept off her troubles.

There was a brief stop for tea and then the coach went on through country that increased steadily in beauty. The air was soft, and the light remarkably clear.

It was late when they reached Beynac. Ferdy brought the *Empress* to a stop at the hotel, a converted château high on a slope above the river. It was to be a two-night stop. The passengers walked up to the driver and thanked him for his excellent driving; Ferdy, beaming, handed the luggage over to the hotel servants and then took the coach round to the garage situated on the other side of the courtyard. Angus reported their arrival to London, checked the list of rooms, distributed the mail and then went upstairs to enjoy the luxury of a bathroom adjoining his room. Emerging fresh and relaxed, he went downstairs again to inspect the tables in the dining-room. The air was so mild that he ordered them carried out on to the wide terrace.

He heard his name, and turned to find Angela coming out of the house. She had changed into a summer dress, and he fingered it and raised an eyebrow.

'Cotton – already?'

'Why not? It's so warm. Have you had the tables put out here?'

'Yes. As you said, it's so warm. Come and sit down.'

They sat at a table and a waiter brought them drinks and then they were alone on the dimly-lit terrace.

'I've just been in father's room,' she said. 'I've been talking to him – about us.'

He stared at her for a moment, and then his head went back and he gave way to unrestrained laughter.

'What's funny?' she asked.

He looked at her.

'You. Didn't we arrange that I was to introduce the topic, tactfully, at dinner tonight?'

'Yes. But whenever you leave me for an instant, I get in a panic.'

'Panic?'

'In case you get away again.'

'What did you tell him?'

'I didn't have to tell him much. He's got eyes. And he's got a sort of fatalistic feeling about this, just as I have. He's always known about my hopeless passion for you, and he's got used to seeing that photograph of you on – '

'*Photograph?*'

'The rugger fifteen. As Captain, you were bang in the middle, but it wasn't a very good likeness. It's been on my dressing table for years. Father said, of course, that he wished you had more. More money, he meant.'

'Did he – '

'Did he what?'

'Did he mention Yule?'

'No. Why should he?'

54

'Because Yule's got a lot to offer, and he's obviously in love with you. I wondered if your father – '

'My father,' she pointed out, 'doesn't regard me as a pewter pot, to be handed to the one with the highest score. I like Lionel, but that's all.' She glanced over Angus's shoulder. 'Father's coming. Will you have any work to do after dinner?'

'Not much. I shall have to go along and see Ferdy.'

'Can I come too?'

'Of course.'

'Then I'll meet you in the garage.'

'That,' said Lord Lorrimer, joining them, 'sounds rather less than romantic.' He looked down at his daughter. 'Wouldn't it be as well,' he asked, 'if I had a word with this young man alone?'

'No. I can't risk it,' she said. 'He's still got a few pockets of resistance, and you might find them. He's keeping a lot of scruples in reserve. I don't trust either of you.'

He smiled, and waved Angus to a chair.

'Let's sit down,' he said. 'But first, let's order drinks.'

When they were brought, he raised his glass with a rather weary smile.

'To headstrong women,' he said. He put his glass down and studied the two young people. 'It's been said before, but I'll say it again: Life plays strange tricks.'

'This isn't a trick,' said Angela. 'This is a reward for single-mindedness. I waited for him, and I got him.'

'I love Angela, and I'd like to marry her, sir,' said Angus. 'I've already told her that I've nothing much to offer her.'

'And she, of course, gave up the whole idea at once?'

'She . . . ' Angus sounded a little hoarse. 'It might not sound much of a future for her, but she says she's prepared to risk it. I feel that she . . . that I . . . I feel – '

'That's what I feel, too,' said Angela.

'There's only one thing I'm not quite certain about,' went on Angus, 'and that is whether she understands that if she marries me, she'll have to make an entirely new life in entirely new conditions.'

'You might do very well in Canada,' said Lord Lorrimer.

'I hope I shall.'

'You're not, Angela tells me, too keen on leaving England?'

'I'm lucky to have a job to go out to, and I'm grateful.'

'But you don't want to go?'

'No.'

'Why not?'

Angus hesitated.

'I . . . It's nothing I can put into words, I'm afraid. My father loved Europe, and so do I. He saw a good deal of it, and so – on Naval leaves – did I. But I only saw a fraction of what I wanted to see. There's . . . there's so much more. I wanted to – I'd planned to write a minor sort of travel history-book; nothing ambitious, just an account of the old battles, the old campaigns, told with photographs of the sites as they are now. The threads of English history . . . you find them woven into so many parts of Europe. Tourists pass old battle-grounds, places where their own kings lived or died, and hardly ever know it. I wanted to . . . I told you it wasn't very easy to explain.'

There was a long silence.

'I don't think,' said Lord Lorrimer slowly at last, 'that you're going to make a very good oil man.'

'I can try.'

'I could perhaps write and put you in touch with one or two people in England who might offer you something.'

'It's very kind of you, sir, but I'm not easy to – to place. We could perhaps discuss it at the end of the journey.'

'Why not now?' asked Angela.

'Because,' answered her father, 'he thinks that you're still pursuing romantic ideas about him.'

'Is that what you think?' she asked Angus.

He smiled.

'No. No, I don't – but I'd like to be quite sure.'

'I came down this evening,' said Lord Lorrimer, after a pause, 'to beg you to keep your heads. But Angus seems to me to be not only keeping his head, but also using it.'

'That's what's wrong with him,' complained Angela. 'He uses it too much.'

Lord Lorrimer did not seem to hear. He was staring out at the darkness beyond the terrace, and when he spoke, it was half to himself.

'You have to grasp happiness when it's offered,' he said slowly. 'It's . . . it's fugitive. You have to take it while you can. If you see a chance now, seize it, for God's sake, and don't let it go.'

They sat in silence. There was a stir inside the house; the diners began to come out on to the terrace, but the three scarcely saw them, for they were busy with their thoughts.

Angus, with Angela's hand touching his own, realised that though she had seemed to travel too swiftly, she had had her own landmarks to guide her. It was true that although he and she had seen little of one another, her interest in him had not been based solely on romantic dreams. She had had a grandstand view of his life; what she had not seen, her brother had relayed to her. If there had been nothing of any special interest to report, there had at least been nothing lurid. She had travelled fast – but she had not travelled in ignorance.

Dinner came, and they ate, but for the most part in silence. Lord Lorrimer's thoughts had gone far away; he seemed lost in sober dreams. When dinner was over, he said good night to the others and went into the house. Mrs Zoller came across to take his place and to talk to Angela, and Angus left them and went to the office to order the variety of breakfasts expected by the passengers.

When he went to say good night to Ferdy, he found that Angela had got there before him and was seated on a long bench in the courtyard, deep in conversation with the driver. The yard was dark, except for the light streaming from the wide doors of the garage and from the room beside it in which Ferdy was to sleep.

'Any likelihood of more bolt-rattling tonight?' Angus asked him.

'Don't think so, sir. I think we've left the snoopers behind. We might get a few of the village lads looking in through the windows, but that's all.'

They watched as he superintended the cleaning of the coach; then they said good night to him and wandered slowly across the courtyard, under the great archway and on to the dark, deserted road. Neither spoke for some time, and when at last Angela broke the silence, her voice sounded quiet and brooding, like the night.

'One thing I can't understand,' she said, 'is why my father said he'd write to his friends about a job for you. Why write? Why not talk to them?'

'One reason is that he isn't in England.'

'But he will be. We're not staying long in Lisbon. He could see people when he goes home, and talk to them about you.'

'Perhaps he feels that my time in England is running short. But, Angela – '

'I know what you're going to say. You don't want him to do

57

anything, because other people have tried, and haven't succeeded. Well, other people weren't my father. When he says
he'll try, it usually means he'll try successfully. Angus, don't
you ever kiss a girl when you take her for a walk along a
wooded path on a dark night?'

'Never. It's asking for trouble. I wait until I've got her
back to the lights.'

'And then?'

'Then I give the briefest salute – like this . . . '

'And then?'

'Then I take her indoors and leave her, as I'm going to
leave you.'

But before he left her, he explained that as she was rather a
special kind of girl, he was prepared to make certain changes.
Taking her in his arms, he demonstrated them – and then they
went in, and he left her and went up to his room and undressed
and lay on his bed looking at a thousand little images of her on
the ceiling. When sleep came at last, it was deep and dreamless.

On the following day, he saw little of the passengers. He and
Angela spent the time together, going out after breakfast with
a picnic lunch and tea, and returning to a late dinner. They
walked by the river, they lay on its banks; the sun was warm,
the country at its best. Angus slept that night as dreamlessly
as he had done the night before, and woke to the hope of
seeing Angela for an hour or two before the coach was due to
leave.

But once more, he had to come down to reality. As he
dressed, a message was brought to him: the driver would like
to see him.

Angus, with a sense of foreboding, finished dressing as
quickly as possible, and went down to the garage. Ferdy met
him with a sober countenance.

'I'm sorry to have sent for you, sir. I thought if I went up
to you, the passengers might see me and feel there was something wrong.'

'What's up, Ferdy?'

'Someone came to the window last night. That window
there. Just daybreak, it was; good time for burglars; they can
see where they're going, but you can't see who they are. I
heard this chap, and I knew he was creeping round to the
garage window, and I thought to m'self: All right, Frenchie,
if you want it, you can have it. So I crept in here, sir, and
waited for him. I was going to wait until he tried to get in, and

then I was going to pull him the rest of the way and shine a torch on him to get a look-see.'

'And – ?'

'It didn't come off, sir. All I got was a whack at him with my torch. Got him on the wrist. I tried to shine the torch on him, but the ruddy switch jammed. I saw his hand and I clutched at it, meaning to drag him in, but he twisted away and all I managed was a crack at the last minute.'

'I wish I'd been here,' said Angus yearningly.

'In a way, I wish you had, sir. We might've got him in, between us. But what I asked you to come down for was to tell you this, sir, and to say I think you ought to report it to the manager. He's on our payroll and he's responsible for the place and I think he ought to have a watchman out at night, on the look-out for prowlers. When this *Empress* goes out, another one comes in; if the chap doesn't get in one night, he might have more luck another time.'

'I'll go and see him now,' said Angus. 'Have you any idea whether it was a young man or an old one?'

'No, sir. If he was an old 'un, he was pretty nippy.'

'I'll speak to the manager,' said Angus, 'but I don't think we'll say anything to the passengers.'

'No, sir. Wouldn't do any good.'

Angus went thoughtfully to the office. It was odd, he reflected, that there had been two attempts, at two different stopping places, to enter the garage. Ferdy had not appeared to attach too much importance to the incidents, but they would have to go down on the report, and Sir Claud would doubtless feel that they were the direct result of breaking his rule and employing an untrained man.

When the passengers were aboard and the coach once more on its way, he would have liked some leisure to think over the matter, but Mrs Denby-Warre came to his compartment and asked to be shown the route they were taking to Lisbon. Angus was surprised by this unusual sign that somebody was aware that the coach was going anywhere, and he proceeded to trace a line across the map.

'We go down – ' he began.

'Down?'

'We go south to – '

'South. Just one moment, please. I always get the points of the compass mixed up. As we're facing now, which is north?'

'Over there.'

'I see. Well, I shall face that way, and then I know that south is behind me and east is on my right hand and – '

'But if you look that way, I'm afraid you won't be able to see the map.'

'Of course not. How silly of me. Where are we at the moment?'

'Just here,' said Angus, pointing to a spot on the map.

'Do you mean to say that in all this time, we've only got as far as that?' she asked in astonishment.

'We've really made quite good time.'

'Oh – *time*! I was speaking of distance.'

Angus struggled on, wondering how a woman could have lived so long and learned so little. On the whole, he decided, he preferred the frankly ignorant to those who, like Mrs Denby-Warre, imagined that they knew a great deal.

When the exhausting session was over, he went into the main part of the coach to get the drinks ready. Carrying them round, he saw the Admiral look down at Maurice Tarrant's hand and give a gruff exclamation.

'Nasty bruise you've got there,' he said.

Maurice, with a quick movement, pulled down his cuff, but Angus, standing over him, had already seen the long, livid mark that covered his wrist.

'How did you get it?' asked the Admiral.

Maurice made a gesture that thanked the Admiral for his sympathy and at the same time waved it aside. He looked up at Angus and took his glass with his left hand.

'How did it happen?' asked Angus slowly.

Maurice met his look with a bland and unruffled air.

'I expect I gave it a knock,' he said. 'Please don't worry about it; it doesn't inconvenience me at all.'

'How did it happen?' repeated Angus.

'I'm not absolutely certain.' Maurice paused and then gave a wide, challenging grin. 'Something hit it, I'm not quite sure what. I rather think, though, that it was a torch.'

CHAPTER 5

FOR the next two hours, Angus's mind was too full of specu-
lation to enable him to devote much attention to the route or
to the passengers. He forced himself to appear as interested
and as helpful as he had been during the earlier part of the
day, but his thoughts were busy supplying possible reasons for
Maurice Tarrant's action.

He wondered what Ferdy would make of it – and decided
that he would say nothing to him until he had spoken to
Tarrant and heard his explanation. He would, he resolved,
try to get Tarrant alone after lunch.

It proved easy. Maurice showed not the slightest desire to
avoid a meeting. Accepting a cigarette from Angus, at whose
table he had lunched, he rose and strolled with apparent
purposelessness out of sight of the other passengers. When
Angus came up to him, he spoke carelessly.

'Not much scenery today, is there?'

Anger flooded Angus, and he waited to get himself under
control. Scenery or not, they were in a part of the country
which he had longed to see again. This was the route which
his father and mother had taken on their honeymoon. Here he
had come with his father, after his mother's death. At Bergerac,
which they had passed not long ago, he had spent more than
one happy holiday by himself. But the passengers, today, had
not been interested in Bergerac; Mr Holt remarked that the
English had once owned it, and the Admiral volunteered the
information that hats were made there.

Now they were in the Landes, which the passengers
thought monotonous, but which to Angus already showed
signs of the Basque country to which they were bound.
Basque farmhouses, timbered and whitewashed, with wide,
sloping roofs, appeared more and more frequently. They
would soon go through Dax, and then they would head
towards Bayonne, where as a small boy he had joined small
Basque boys and played pelota, in defiance of prohibitions,
against the walls of the medieval cathedral. All these things,
all these memories should have been filling his mind – but it
was occupied, instead, in trying to read what lay behind
Maurice Tarrant's untroubled countenance.

'Before we talk about scenery,' he began, 'perhaps you'd care to explain how you got that bruise on your wrist.'

'But I told you, my dear fellow.' Maurice raised his eyebrows in surprise. 'I hit it against something – a torch, I imagine.'

'Can you explain why you were trying to get into the garage early this morning?'

Maurice appeared to consider.

'Couldn't we put it down to a boyish prank?' he asked finally.

'I don't think so.' Angus, with an effort, spoke quietly. 'You tried the bolts of the door and – '

'No – cross my heart,' said Maurice, with obvious sincerity. 'I didn't touch the bolts of the door at any time.'

'But you did try to climb in through the window last night?'

'Purely for exercise. I couldn't sleep, and I thought that a spot of climbing would, so to speak, make me drop off. If I'd known the driver slept so close to his baby, I – '

' – would have thought twice about trying to get at it.'

'I wouldn't even have thought once,' said Maurice earnestly. 'A great, heavy chap like that – consider, my dear fellow! Is it likely I'd risk letting him have a bash at me?'

'Will you please tell me what you were after?'

'You don't believe I was merely taking exercise?'

Angus thrust his hands deep into his pockets.

'Look, Tarrant,' he said. 'I'm responsible for the safety of the passengers and – '

'Safety? You don't for a moment imagine, do you, that I would have done anything to harm any of them?'

'Then what were you after?'

'Nothing but adventure. Why should I want to do anything to put the coach out of action? I'm a passenger too, you know, and I'm as keen to get to Lisbon as any of the others. And I'd like to get there in one piece.'

'If you ever hang round the coach again out of travel hours,' Angus warned him, 'you'll get there in several pieces.'

He turned and walked away; there was no point in prolonging the discussion. Tarrant had his reasons and was obviously not going to disclose them; all that could be done was maintain a stricter watch when the *Empress* was put away for the night.

Miss Seton and Lionel Yule strolled back to the coach with him.

'Do we stop at Biarritz?' she asked him.

'No. We go through it and along the coast for a bit, and then we turn inland and stop for the night at a place just this side of Sare.'

'And tomorrow, Spain?'

'Yes. How's your Spanish?'

'Negligible.'

'What route do we take after San Sebastian?' asked Lionel.

'We make first for Pamplona, by way of Estrella, Logrono and Najera,' Angus told him.

'That's not the main road, is it?'

'It's the route the pilgrims used to take in the Middle Ages,' said Angus, and repressed a strong impulse to tell him that what was good enough for Charlemagne should be good enough for him.

As the coach moved on once more, he sat thinking about the garage episode, but he found it impossible to guess what business Tarrant could have had with the *Green Empress*, and found himself wondering at last whether it could not be put down to another example of his undeveloped idea of fun.

When the coach left the coast road near St Jean de Luz and turned inland, the good weather left them and a drizzling rain began to fall. They were to stop for tea at a Basque farmhouse a mile or two off the main road, and as they drew near to it, the downpour became so heavy that Angus took the coats from the cupboard and handed them round to their owners. When the coach stopped, they draped the coats round them and ran quickly across the few yards between the coach and the house.

Inside, the room was rather dark, smoke-filled, and smelt strongly of wine. The arrival of the party caused a smiling stir, and the stout farmer and his wife and several small children came to greet them.

Soon the passengers were seated at small tables; Mr and Mrs Zoller sat with Mrs Denby-Warre, while the Admiral and Lord Lorrimer took a table beside a window. Angus stood talking to the farmer; he could see Angela seated on a bench at a long table; beside her on one side was Maurice Tarrant, talking volubly; on the other side was Lionel Yule, talking not at all.

Close by, he could hear Mr Holt's deep, drawling voice addressing Miss Seton.

'Back home,' he was saying, 'I've got a reputation for being quite a thought-reader. Want to know how I've been reading yours?'

His voice was as easy and as relaxed as his posture; he was sitting forward on his low wooden chair, his feet outstretched, his arms resting on the table.

'I didn't know I'd been thinking at all,' she said.

'I've been watching you, and I think you've been thinking,' said Mr Holt. He took off his glasses, polished them, put them on again and gave her a direct, thoughtful gaze. 'You got bad news on the trip, didn't you?'

'Did I?'

'Well, I'm asking you. You don't have to tell me if you don't want to. All I'm doing is proving to you what I said in the first place: that I can get a lot of information just by watching somebody and figuring out what's going on inside their heads. First you were happy, and then you weren't. Am I right?'

'Yes. But does it matter?'

'Of course it matters. Why would a person bother watching another person unless that first person wanted to do what he could to help the other person – if the other person would let him?'

Miss Seton stared at him for a few moments, and then laughed.

'So I'm funny,' agreed Mr Holt placidly, 'but I'm talking good sense.'

'You're being very kind,' said Miss Seton, sobering, 'but do you honestly think that two complete strangers can – '

'Oh, but wait a minute!' Mr Holt held up a hand for silence. 'Wait a minute, now. Take this slowly. We're no strangers. We've been living together for three and a half days and if you parcel out the time we've spent together, you could spread it out over a whole lot of years of ordinary getting-to-know-you. I think you've taken a knock and I like the way you've taken it, and all I'm saying is that perhaps I could help you. I'm forty-three years old and I've led a busy life and I've moved around and I guess that a lot of the things that have hit other people have hit me too – so how do you know that I haven't had this trouble that you've got now? Everybody has the same troubles. Your parents die; so do mine. Other people lose money; I lose money. Other people make fools of themselves; I do it all the time. So you see? Your troubles are my troubles.'

There was a pause. Miss Seton seemed about to speak, and changed her mind.

'One of the first things you said to me,' Mr Holt reminded her, 'was that I had a lot of courage. Well, I think you've got a lot of courage, too. That makes two of us, and the more I think of the two of us . . . What's your first name?'

'Caroline.'

'Caroline.' He sounded pleased. 'That's a nice name, and it suits you. Could I use it?'

Angus moved out of earshot, wondering whether the cool, self-possessed Miss Seton would find herself having to deal with more than one problem on the journey. He felt that Mr Holt was a man who, once embarked upon a project, would work hard to bring it to a successful conclusion.

One by one, the passengers rose and strolled back to the waiting coach. The rain had stopped and a fitful sun was shining. Mrs Denby-Warre distributed small change to a group of brown-faced children who had gathered at the side of the road, and remarked that she would give a lot to see a plump, clear-skinned English child.

'Stronger than they look, these children,' her brother told her. 'They're tough.'

'They may be tough – ' began Mrs Denby-Warre, and stopped. Lionel Yule, who had entered the coach behind Angela, was now standing on the step looking pale and almost panic-stricken. His eyes sought out Angus, and he spoke in an agitated voice.

'My . . . my despatch case. It's gone.'

'Gone?'

'I left it on the seat when I got out of the coach. It's – it's gone.'

Without answering, Angus walked forward and boarded the coach.

'It was there, on my seat, and it isn't there now.'

'Is it in your locker?' asked Angus.

'No. I looked.'

Ferdy's form appeared in the doorway.

'Anything wrong, sir?'

'Mr Yule has mislaid his despatch case.'

'In which,' added Lionel, 'there are a number of very important documents.' He glanced across at Lord Lorrimer, and the latter spoke quietly.

'Papers which wouldn't,' he said, 'be of much use or

interest – and certainly of no value – to thieves. I think they must merely be mislaid.'

'I was working on them an hour ago,' said Lionel, 'and I intended to take them up to my room tonight and finish off a few notes. When I got up to leave the coach, I put the case on my seat.'

'If that's so' – it was Miss Seton's voice; she had stepped into the coach and Angus was grateful for the coolness of her words and manner – 'if that's so, it probably slipped down somewhere and somebody may have picked it up and put it in another place – or in one of the lockers for safety.'

She began to move from one locker to the next, beginning at the Admiral's and moving up the aisle, opening the doors and peering inside. Mr Holt, who had followed her into the coach, conducted a search on the opposite side.

'Not a sign of it,' he reported at the end.

'Nor this side,' said Miss Seton.

Angus was turning out the contents of the cupboard. Ferdy was on his knees searching the floor and thrusting his hand deep into the space behind the cushions of the seats. At the end of the search, there was nothing to report but failure.

'It isn't here, sir,' said Ferdy, getting to his feet and brushing his trousers.

'Could it have dropped off the coach?' suggested Miss Seton.

They were all waiting uneasily, some in, some out of the coach. The group of children drew near and the Admiral waved them away, shooing them before him like a flock of geese.

'Are you sure you didn't take it in with you when you went into the farmhouse?' he returned to ask Lionel.

'I left it on my seat,' reiterated Lionel firmly. 'I put it down, draped my coat round me to keep off the rain, and walked out of the coach.'

'Who came out after you?' asked Angus.

'I did, for one,' said Mr Holt.

'Did you see the case?'

'No, I didn't – but I don't think I happened to look over to that side of the coach. Come to think of it, I threw my coat over my head, kind of like an umbrella, and made a dash for it.'

'I came out after Mr Holt,' said Miss Seton. 'I was the last but one.

66

'And I was the last,' said Maurice.

'Did you see the case?'

'Yes, I did,' he answered without hesitation. 'It was lying on the seat. I saw it as I left my own seat, which is almost opposite Yule's. Are you sure,' he asked Lionel, 'that you didn't have a feeling you oughtn't to have left it there, and went back to fetch it?'

'I didn't go back to the coach,' said Lionel.

Angus turned to Ferdy.

'Could anybody have got into the coach while we were away from it?'

'If they did, sir, it was a quick job,' said Ferdy. 'I got out as soon as I pulled up, and I went inside and had a quick wash; then I walked up and down, giving my legs a stretch, rain or no rain, and then you sent me out some tea and I had it sitting at that table out there under that bit of shelter. Apart from the time I was having a wash, sir, I had the *Empress* in view the whole time. What's more, I was coming out of the building just as you all was going in, and I saw Mr Holt and Miss Seton and Mr Tarrant getting off.'

'Which means that nobody could have entered the coach without your seeing them,' said the Admiral.

'They could've crept round, I suppose, sir, and nipped in, but I'm sure I should've seen them.'

'Then we'll all go and look inside the farmhouse,' said the Admiral.

Mr Holt fell into step beside Angus and spoke a few words inaudible to the others.

'Maybe somebody went back and fetched it out of the coach,' he said. 'You get jokers, remember, in every pack.'

The despatch case was not in the room, not in the coach, not in the roadway. Angus, after checking statements, movements, and exploring every possibility, spoke regretfully to Lord Lorrimer.

'I'm very sorry, but I'm afraid it can't be found.'

'Don't worry,' Lord Lorrimer sounded unmoved. 'It'll turn up, perhaps. Perhaps you'd better explain to the farmer that the papers have no value, but if the case is brought to him and he sends it on, I'll pay a small reward for its return.'

'Shouldn't it be reported to the police?' asked Maurice.

'No. There's no need for that,' said Lord Lorrimer. 'And I suggest' – he turned to Angus – 'that there's nothing to keep us here. The case has gone.'

Angus went back to explain the matter to the farmer, and then followed the passengers on to the coach. When they were on their way, Angela came to sit beside him.

'Worried?' she asked.

'A little. I shall have to report it, and it makes another smudge on my career as a courier.'

'It wasn't your fault.'

'No, but it's my responsibility. I may only be a fill-in, but I was growing rather fond of this *Empress*, and I was looking forward to doing the two journeys – out and back – without a black mark showing anywhere.'

'Don't take it too seriously. Lionel's all right, but he likes to give the impression that nobody's ever carried such a heavy weight of work before. The papers weren't important; you heard my father say so.'

'Important or not, they were part of a passenger's luggage, and I'm supposed to deliver the personnel and the packages intact.'

'Stop worrying, and think of something else. Would you say we had a romance aboard?'

'Miss Seton and Holt?'

'Then I'm not imagining it?'

'I don't think so. But don't see too much; it might just be that they're being thrown together.'

'And he might have several wives in the States.'

'There's no wife on his passport – not that that proves anything. If he did have one, I think he's the type who'd say so. Perhaps – '

There was an interruption. Mrs Denby-Warre had come, she told them, to make a suggestion about the missing case.

'Only a suggestion,' she repeated, taking Angus's seat. 'I've been thinking it over, and I'm wondering if it isn't one of those instances of mass hypnotism. We got used to seeing Mr Yule working at his papers, and so today, we imagined that he was still working. It's quite possible, you know.'

There was a pause.

'You mean,' said Angela at last, 'that the case hasn't been on the coach at all today, and is somewhere else?'

'In Mr Yule's luggage, most probably. He forgot to bring the despatch case into the coach with him this morning.'

'Well, we haven't long to wait before getting to the hotel,' pointed out Angus. 'Then we can see if – '

'See? One cannot always see,' broke in Mrs Denby-Warre. 'Do you know much about the Occult?'

It being clear that they did not, she favoured them with a brief talk and then, her enthusiasm kindled, went back to her seat to raise the subject with the other passengers.

'What do you make of that?' asked Angela, when she had gone.

'She's wise to stick to lemonade.'

'Do you think she believes it all?'

'I've no idea. Is she giving the lecture again in there?'

'I think so. She's full of odd ideas.'

'Ideas? Her mind's full of cobwebs; she hasn't used it since she left school – and she didn't use it much when she was there. What,' he enquired, 'made me think that people go on trips like this to see and to learn?'

'That's just your courier blood. You're still looking depressed.'

'I feel depressed. I feel depressed about us. I've got a shaky feeling. A feeling that I'm just dreaming it all.'

'I've got that feeling too, but it doesn't make me shake. It's a nice feeling. After all, this *is* a dream, isn't it? Love's young?'

'When you're sitting here beside me, it's all right. When you're not with me – '

'You begin to shake? You needn't. If you have any fear that you'll wake up and find I've vanished, you can put it out of your mind. You've got me for ever and ever.'

He looked at her.

'Haven't you ever loved anyone else?'

'Never. I've told you. I saw what I wanted – you.'

'But if we hadn't met on this trip . . . '

'We did meet. If Mrs Denby-Warre knew the circumstances, she'd say you weren't here at all and that I was just imagining you were. What's tonight's hotel like?'

'A bit out in the blue. Nowhere to go – but we could walk after dinner, if you felt like it.'

When they reached the hotel, his first move, after completing the usual formalities, was to change his room and take the one next to the driver's.

'All you've got to do,' he told Ferdy, when he said good night to him, 'is to bang on the wall, and I'll wake,'

'Don't suppose anything'll happen, sir,' said Ferdy, with a touch of regret in his voice. 'But if it does, we ought to do some damage: you've got the reach and I've got the weight. Any sign of that despatch case, sir?'

'None.'

'Funny business,' mused Ferdy. 'Got any ideas, sir?'

'Not one. The more I think about it, the less I know about it.'

He left him and went in search of Angela. In spite of what he had just told Ferdy, he had one idea about the missing despatch case, and that was that Maurice Tarrant must be in some way involved in its disappearance. But he had no proof, and at this moment he had no mind to look for any; he had been compelled throughout dinner to listen to Mrs Denby-Warre's conversation, and that was duty enough for one evening. He would find Angela and they would go out for some exercise.

As he was about to leave his room, there was a knock on the door, and it opened to admit Lionel Yule.

'Oh, you're going out,' he said. 'I don't want to keep you.'

'You're not keeping me. What can I do for you?' asked Angus.

Lionel closed the door and advanced into the room.

'About the despatch case – ' he began.

'We've – '

'I know. You've made a thorough search, and I'm grateful. I didn't come to ask whether you'd found it; I wanted to ask if you had any ideas . . . any theories as to who'd taken it. Because, of course, somebody did take it. I'm not a careless man; I wouldn't be holding this job if I were. It was wrong, I know now, to leave it on the seat, but I knew that nobody would be in the coach for the next half hour or more, and so I thought I could risk it. I thought it would be safe – and it would have been, if we'd kept an eye on Tarrant. I'm quite convinced that he had something to do with it.'

'Why would he take it?'

'Because his chief interest in life seems to be annoying people, and for some reason he's picked me as his chief victim. One of the reasons I worked on those papers was to avoid having to listen to him – and I think he knows it. And so he took the case, and I'd be grateful if you'd tackle him about it. You can do it officially and I can't.'

'I've tried once to get something out of Tarrant that he wants to keep to himself. It's wasted labour, but I'll have another go in the morning.'

'Can't you do it tonight?'

'I'm afraid not.'

There was a pause. Angus waited for the other man to tell him that the well-being of the passengers came before evening walks, and while he waited, he studied him and found an unexpected feeling of sympathy welling up in him. It couldn't be easy, he thought, to watch Angela going out of reach. He marvelled at Yule's unvarying courtesy; he looked a normal man, and a normal man's instincts in a situation of this kind were surely to exterminate his rival – but Yule's manner showed nothing but politeness.

'If you like,' Angus offered impulsively, 'I'll go along now and say something to him.'

'No.' Lionel spoke gloomily. 'I can see it wouldn't be any use. He'd deny it, and then he'd reduce it to the level of one of his crack-brained jokes. No; leave it. If you'll watch him and jump on him the moment you feel you've any proof that he had something to do with it . . .'

'I'll do that on my own account as well as on yours. It's easy to have too much of Tarrant.'

Yule went to the door and then turned.

'I suppose one shouldn't say it at this stage,' he said, 'but about you and Angela . . . if congratulations are in order . . .'

'Thank you.'

'You've been a bit of a stumbling block for years, but I put it down to the uniform, and I didn't feel you'd ever materialise. I thought it would wear off – especially if she met you again. I didn't take it at all seriously. My sisters used to do the same thing – sigh over fellows' photographs. I thought it was a phase all girls had to go through. I was wrong – in this case, anyway.' He opened the door. 'I hope you'll both be very happy.'

The door closed, and Angus was left staring at it. Good breeding? he wondered. Cold blood? Or what was known as civilised behaviour?

If it was civilisation, it was civilisation, he decided, in its highest form.

CHAPTER 6

EARLY next morning, Angus was summoned to Lord Lorrimer's room. He was already dressed, and he went at once, arriving at the door at the same moment as the maid who was carrying in coffee and *brioches*. Lord Lorrimer, standing at a table in a dressing gown, said nothing until she had put down the tray and gone out; then he turned to Angus.

'I'm sorry to disturb you so early – but I see that you were already up. I had something to show you.'

He opened a cupboard. From it he took the missing despatch case. Holding it, he looked at Angus, and for some moments there was silence.

'The papers, too?' asked Angus at last.

'Everything intact. The papers, as I told you, were of no importance. The case was just inside the door when I got up this morning. Someone had obviously opened the door a few inches, pushed the case in – and departed.' He smiled. 'If it were worth it, we could get a few fingerprints, but I feel that the best thing to do is write it off as a very poor practical joke.'

'Which points to Tarrant,' said Angus, and frowned.

'You feel he's too obvious a suspect?'

'In a way. At the same time, if he was merely trying to annoy Yule – '

'Practical jokers don't mind being found out; doesn't it rather add to their idea of fun?'

'I suppose so, sir. I'm sorry it happened.'

'Perhaps Lionel asked for it. He showed pretty clearly that he thought Tarrant was a damned idiot. I sympathise with him, but when you're shut up in a coach with one of these irritating types, you have to make the best of it. If you'll announce the return of the case when we're over the frontier, I'll give them all a plausible explanation; that might stop any gossip.' He paused with the coffee pot in his hand. 'I hope you've had yours?'

'Yes, thank you.'

'What time do we start this morning?'

'Eleven, sir. Lunch at Pamplona.'

'And after that, a two-night stop in Burgos?'

'Yes. Time for the passengers' – he smiled – 'to do a bit of serious sight-seeing.'

Lord Lorrimer stirred his coffee and smiled in sympathy. 'You don't find us responsive travellers ?'

Unresponsive, thought Angus, was perhaps the word. Lord Lorrimer had his mind on something else, Yule had his nose in his papers, Mr Zoller was asleep and his wife filling books with car numbers, like a ten-year-old schoolboy. The Admiral was unresponsive to travel as a whole and his sister . . .

'Not too responsive, sir,' he said.

He went to the door, and heard Lord Lorrimer call him.

'Angus.'

It was the first time he had used the name. Surprised, Angus turned to find the old man staring at him with a strangely fixed expression.

'Sir ?'

He waited. The silence lengthened and he saw that though Lord Lorrimer's gaze was on him, he was looking beyond him at something else. Angus knew that a struggle was going on; he had been called back to hear something – something important; something, he felt certain, that would explain Lord Lorrimer's preoccupation. He was . . . he wasn't . . . he was about to speak.

And then, with a slight shake of the head, the older man came to himself and Angus knew that the moment had passed. The impulse had gone. He was going to say nothing.

He walked thoughtfully back to his room. Putting away his instructions on France and getting out those relative to Spain, he studied them and wondered whether this particular *Green Empress* journey could be said by Sir Claud to be going according to plan. He had refused to accept the word courier, and had stressed that his young men were liaison officers – but what was needed more than a liaison officer on this trip, reflected Angus, was a detective, an elementary schoolmaster and a psychiatrist.

He walked to the window and stood looking out at the view, trying to fix it for ever in his mind. The Basque country. There would be more of it on the other side of the border.

Spain. If he loved France for the memories it evoked, Spain bred in him an excitement that was of the senses. The music, the language, the land itself with its dramatic contrasts of softness and starkness . . . soon he would be seeing it again, and seeing it, this time, with Angela.

73

He thought of the day's run, and gloom descended on him as he reflected that nobody on the coach would be in the smallest degree interested in Burgos. The Admiral might recall that cellophane was made there, and somebody might remember, vaguely, that it had some connection with the English Queen Eleanor, who had some connection with Charing Cross, but for the most part, they would be completely – yes, there was the word again – unresponsive. They would chatter about the despatch case, argue about the Occult.

At eleven o'clock, he saw the passengers aboard, and the coach moved towards the frontier. When they reached Hendaye, he found, as he had found on their entry into France, that formalities were reduced to a minimum. The passengers got out and strolled to and fro, changing money and buying souvenirs; as they drove on to Spanish soil, they passed a *Green Empress* on its way to France; there was a pause, an exchange of courtesies and then Ferdy drove on once more in the direction of Pamplona.

Angus explained to the passengers that as they were now to adopt the Spanish times for meals, lunch would not be until three o'clock, and dinner at ten; they would therefore halt at a *tasca* at about one o'clock and eat and drink a little to stave off hunger before the late lunch hour.

'Play hell with my digestion,' grumbled the Admiral. 'Oily food's bad enough, but oily food at three in the afternoon and ten at night . . . '

Mrs Zoller thought that in this weather, so hot, one did not wish to eat anything.

'It is pleasant, no ?' she asked the Admiral.

He did not think so. He had ascertained that the warm weather was general over Europe, and his mind was on his garden at home, left in charge of a day-a-week man on whom he placed not the smallest reliance.

'This'll bring on the raspberries,' he mourned, 'and I shan't be there to pick 'em. That fellow's been told to put the sprinkler on the lawn if there's a heat wave, but he won't. He won't do anything. I'll go back to find the whole place under weeds.'

'Can't you stop thinking about your garden ?' asked his sister with a touch of irritation.

'No, I can't. I put in several hundred hours getting it into shape, and if I don't keep it in shape, it'll run away from me and I shall never get it right again. I'm too old to do all that donkey work I did before.'

'You are old, yes,' said Mrs Zoller with her usual tact, 'but you can have gardeners, no?'

'No,' said the Admiral shortly, and grew purple with the effort of preventing himself from adding that only bloated millionaires could have gardeners at four shillings an hour, six days a week. He settled himself angrily in his seat, shook open the English newspaper he had bought at the frontier, and hid himself behind it.

'Incidentally,' said Angus, to the passengers in general, as he went back to his compartment, 'I'm glad to tell you that Mr Yule's despatch case has been found.'

'Found?' The Admiral lowered his paper. 'Found where?'

Lord Lorrimer answered the question.

'Mr Graham and the driver found it on the coach when they were able to make a thorough search. Mr Graham brought it to my room last night.' He handed the case to Lionel. 'It must have got wedged behind the seat,' he said.

Lionel, without a word, took the case and put it into his locker. Leaving them all to discuss the matter if they wished, Angus went back to his compartment and looked out at the sunlit scenery. His mind was on Angela, and soon she came to join him.

'Why didn't you tell me about the case?' she asked in surprise.

'I wasn't sure what your father was going to say about it.'

'How did it get back?'

'Somebody – probably Tarrant – pushed it just inside his room during the night. Have the others swallowed your father's version?'

'Apparently. All except Mr Holt and Miss Seton. Mr Holt gazed out of the window one side, and she gazed out the other side and they both looked – '

'Sceptical?'

'No. Purposely blank.'

'Well, that's that. See the yoke on that ox-cart? I've got one. My father made it into the the back of a garden seat, and it looks good. They're heavy, but the decoration's interesting.'

'Have you seen Roncesvalles?'

'Yes. Have you?'

'Yes.'

'Which was the last army to march through there?'

'Bonaparte's. And the Black Prince went through there. And Charlemagne's rearguard was destroyed there and Roland died there and he blew three blasts on his magic horn called . . . called something or other. Olivant. You thought I didn't know anything, didn't you?'

'I didn't know; I only feared.'

'This Roland character had a magic sword too. If he had a magic sword, how did he manage to get killed?'

'He ought to have swapped it for a magic suit of armour. Do you know as many facts about Burgos?'

'I don't know one. I've never been there.'

'Good. Then I can show it to you. It's beautiful. Will you come out to dinner with me?'

'I'll think about it.'

'And when you've thought about it?'

'I'll come out to dinner with you.'

She stayed with him until they reached Pamplona. In spite of the one o'clock stop, most of the passengers were hungry and some a little peevish by three. Angus ordered sherry as they waited for the meal, but the Admiral refused it; eating at that hour was bad enough, he said, but drinking was worse.

Mr Holt and Miss Seton had withdrawn a little from the rest. Lord Lorrimer sat with Lionel Yule; the Zollers joined Mrs Denby-Warre. As usual, Mr Zoller was silent; when addressed, he answered as briefly as possible and relapsed into silence once more. People seldom approached him, for he was as sharp as his wife was stupid, and on the few occasions on which his small, beady eyes were open, he let them roam, hard and unblinking, from one of his fellow-passengers to the other, studying them, missing nothing.

Maurice went to sit beside Angela. He mentioned the Pamplona bull-running, and soon a heated argument on bull-fighting was taking place.

'But have you ever seen one? A good one, I mean,' said Maurice.

'Yes, I have,' said Angela. 'I saw one in Madrid with all the top toreadors and – '

'Toreros.'

'Who cares? It was horrible.'

'Cold-blooded slaughter,' said the Admiral.

'My dear Admiral' – Maurice's voice was edged with contempt – 'there's nothing in the least cold-blooded about bull-fighting. If you'd understood what was going on – '

76

'I understood everything that was going on,' said the Admiral, his colour deepening dangerously. 'They were slaughtering the bull, that's what was going on.'

'But if you'd watched with real knowledge – ' said Maurice.

'Oh, I have heard all that,' said Mrs Zoller. 'All that, my husband told me. Watch this matador, he said; watch how he does this with his hat and this with his feet, and this with his cape. But all the time, I watch the bull and – '

'Well, that was a mistake,' said Maurice. 'If you're going to miss all the – '

'Yes, yes, yes,' broke in the Admiral angrily, 'we know all about that. Twenty-five different dance steps or something of that kind. But that's only when the bull's had a lance driven into it and is half dead. Do they do twenty-five dance steps when the bull's fully alive? They do not. A lot of fellows in pink stockings and silly hats flick their capes at the bull and then run hell for leather into those little wooden boxes at the side of the ring. None of your dance steps then, you mark my words. None of your slow tangos round the bull. They keep those till the animal's half dead. What d'you say?' he asked Lord Lorrimer.

'The great mistake,' said Lord Lorrimer, 'lies in calling it a fight. The Spanish don't. Their word is *corrida*, which means a race or a sprint.'

'And how they sprint!' said the Admiral. 'Until the bull's dying on its feet. And bull-fighting was dying on its feet, too, until that writer chap wrote a book that started this vogue for pretending to know all about the finer points. Finer points, pah!'

'I agree,' said Lord Lorrimer, 'that football is slowly but surely superseding – '

'Never,' said Maurice, never averse to interrupting his elders. 'What do you think?' he asked Angus.

Angus shook his head.

'Religion, politics – and bull-fighting,' he said.

'See what you mean,' said the Admiral. 'Quite right. Gets you nowhere.'

Lunch was announced and they went in eagerly, and for the rest of the afternoon took little interest in the landscape. The coach went on; Burgos was ahead and excitement rose in Angus. He remembered its beautiful buildings, and remembered also that Wax had told him that Sir Claud had restored an old Renaissance palace and made it into a *Green Empress* hotel.

They reached the outskirts of the city and drove slowly through the *plaza*, crowded with gay girls and soldiers from the garrison; the white cotton gloves worn by every soldier made the travellers, in some obscure way, conscious for the first time of being in the real Spain. Ferdy threaded his way through narrow streets and stopped at last before the hotel, and three small, dark, uniformed pages tumbled down the steps and stood smilingly at the coach door, waiting for the passengers to alight.

The luggage was carried out and placed in the hall. Angus went forward to meet the manager, who was called Señor Portalas and who was grave and polite and whose eyes, dark, spaniel-like, lit with homage when they rested upon Angela.

'*Guapa!*' he murmured reverently to Angus, ushering him into the office.

'*Guapa* indeed,' agreed Angus inwardly.

Rooms were ready. Soon, baths were flowing. Dinner was still two hours away, but in the meantime there was sherry, dry, pale gold.

And the others could do what they liked, Angus decided, without the help of a courier. He was going to take Angela out to dinner.

They went out early, and on foot. They strolled slowly along the lighted streets, only half aware of their surroundings. They stopped to look at the windows of still-open shops, and the proprietors came to the doors and looked at Angus with hope lighting a gleam in their eyes.

'Americano?'

'No.'

Hope died, to revive once more when Angela went inside and fingered delicate black lace mantillas and draped them over her fair hair. Angus bought one for her, as frail as a cobweb.

'When will you wear it?' he asked her, smiling.

'To church.' Her voice was dreamy. 'I'll wear a black suit, unrelieved, and I'll go into church late and walk up to the family pew, past all the feathers and summer felts and straw-with-flowers. I shall look remote, and tragic, and the vicar will forget what he was going to preach about.'

'He might decide to preach about exhibitionism instead.'

He was fingering some scarves, and he drew out a small

one and held it out to see if the colour suited her. He bought it with the mantilla, and while the latter was being wrapped, Angela made the scarf into a narrow band and tied it round her hair.

'You like that?'

'I like that,' he said.

They strolled out of the shop, and she looked up at him.

'You think it's just a scarf,' she said slowly, 'but it's more than that. It's a – a symbol. A talisman. No, it's a signal. Whenever I wear it, in all the years we're together, it'll mean that I love you especially much. I shan't have to give out any heavy hints at the breakfast table on the morning of our anniversaries; I shall just sit down and pour out your coffee, and you'll look up and see that I'm wearing this scarf with the tiny fans all over it, and you'll know you've forgotten to buy me an anniversary present.'

They were at the door of a restaurant in a narrow, un-savoury street. She paused and looked dubiously at the low, dark doorway.

'Is this a suitable place to bring a delicately-reared girl?' she wanted to know.

'They feed you magnificently.'

'Lead on,' she commanded.'

They sat at a corner table; he bought her a *bota* and filled it with wine and she put her head back and tried, unsuccess-fully, and to the amusement of the other diners, to direct the scarlet stream down her throat.

'No good,' said Angus. 'You do it this way.'

'Where did you learn?'

'Here. Where else? Drink your wine.'

'What is it?'

'Logrono. Like it?'

'Yes.'

'Then drink it and let's get away by ourselves somewhere.'

They went back to the hotel at last as they had left it – on foot, strolling easily and for the most part in silence. Angus kissed her good night in the hall of their palace, hoping that the pillars would shield them from the bright, curious gaze of the sole page on duty. He held her in his arms, and released her at last and looked down at her.

'And so I bring you to my castle,' he said. 'By courtesy of Sir Claud.'

His hands were in hers, and she swung them gently to and fro.

79

'I've been making up some beautiful, moving poetry,' she told him. 'Want to hear it?'

'Please.'

'Well, it starts off:

> Angus and Angela dined out in Spain.
> "Will you," he asked her, "come with me again?" '

She paused. 'You are going to ask me, I suppose?'

'I daresay. Is that the end?'

'No. I'll begin again, and then you can hear it as a beautiful whole:

> Angus and Angela dined out in Spain.
> "Will you," he asked her, "come with me again?"
> "Sir," she replied, "with a man of your worth
> I would go – if you asked – to the ends of the earth."

There was a pause.

'Like it?' she asked.

He tried to speak, and found that he could not. The absurd little rhyme, spoken in her light, soft voice, conveyed as no serious lines could have done her love and her trust in him. They stood looking at one another, and then he raised one of her hands and kissed it gently.

'Thank you, Miss Clunes, for the happiest night of my life.'

'Thank you, Mr Graham, for the most wonderful night of mine. Dear Mr Graham,' she said dreamily, 'how I long, how I long for the time when we won't have to part for the night . . .'

He left her, lingeringly, reluctantly, at the door of her room and went to his, to dream of her. Dawn was breaking when he fell asleep.

But once again, he had to wake to cold reality – and to one hard and unpleasant fact.

Maurice Tarrant's luggage – all of it – had disappeared.

CHAPTER 7

THE details were soon learned. Maurice had dined with Mr and Mrs Zoller. They had gone on to a cinema which began at eleven-thirty and ended shortly before two in the morning. They had returned to the hotel and Maurice had gone straight to his room, which was next to that of the Zollers. He had had a bath and gone to bed. Tired after the day's drive and the evening's pleasure, he had slept heavily. When he awakened, it was to find that his large suitcase, his small suitcase and their contents had vanished, together with the clothes and even the shoes that had been lying about the room. A search had been made, without result. At the end of the search and the questioning and the confusion of suggestion and counter-suggestion, one fact remained unchanged: the luggage was missing.

'But why do they take yours?' Mrs Zoller wanted to know. 'Why do they not take mine? Mine is of more value. My jewels by themselves, they are more worth stealing, and my clothes, and my shoes. Why do they not take those?'

'There were two of you in the room,' pointed out the Admiral. 'But how,' he went on, addressing Maurice, in whose bedroom they were all gathered, 'how the devil could anybody enter a room and remove two cases without disturbing you?'

'When I'm asleep,' said Maurice, 'somebody could remove the bed without disturbing me.'

'Are there only two bedrooms on this floor?' asked Mr Holt.

'Yes. Mine, and the Zollers'. If I'm a heavy sleeper,' said Maurice, 'then so are they, because for all the good that wall is for keeping out sound, you might as well take it down and put up a curtain. The outer walls of this place might be ten feet thick, but the inner ones must be made of plaster. I could hear them moving and I could hear them talking before I went to sleep. I could almost hear them undressing. So if there was a gang of porters in my room in the early hours, carting off my effects, I think it's odd the Zollers didn't hear anything.'

Angus left them to argue, and went downstairs to the office, to give orders that the police were to be informed of what had taken place. He kept his manner calm, but his mind was heavy with depression.

Four days – four incidents. Somebody had tried the bolts of the garage door; Maurice Tarrant had attempted to enter the garage. Lionel Yule's despatch case had vanished – and reappeared. And now somebody had stolen Maurice Tarrant's luggage – and while it had seemed likely that he might have had something to do with the disappearance of the despatch case, it was impossible to imagine him stealing his own luggage.

The incidents, which so far Angus had tended to regard as

merely irritating, now began to assume a more serious aspect. If his own job, he mused, had been a permanent one, he would almost have suspected that somebody was working very hard to bring about his dismissal. The history of the *Green Empresses* had not been written, but he doubted whether any incidents of this kind had ever taken place on one of the leisurely, carefully-planned runs. One mishap would have been regrettable; four were altogether too much. Nobody, not even Sir Claud, could say that he could be held to blame for any of them, but the incidents, and his own inexperience, would be bracketed and the inevitable conclusion drawn.

He would not have thought, a week ago, that he would have been so depressed at the thought of disappointing Sir Claud. The job had looked easy and he had undertaken it without misgiving. And now . . .

He went outside, to find Ferdy downcast and obviously bewildered. He had little to say about the affair, but it was clear that he was thinking that upsets of this kind had never before occurred to mar the smooth progress of a trip.

Passing through the hall on his way upstairs, Angus saw Maurice talking to Mr Holt. After a moment's hesitation, he walked up to them and addressed Tarrant.

'I don't need to tell you – personally as well as officially – that I'm sorry this has happened.'

Maurice waved a hand.

'Not your fault, my dear fellow. No blame attached to you or to the Company.'

'Their rule,' Angus told him, 'is to cover passengers' losses on the route, so if you'll give me a list of – '

'We were just talking about that, Holt and I,' Maurice broke in. 'He's just offered me dollars in return for a sterling cheque, so that I could get myself some replacements.'

'That was kind, and I'm grateful,' said Angus, 'but the Company will take care of it.'

' 'Tisn't money that's needed, thanks all the same,' said Maurice. 'It's time I want. I can buy a suit off the peg, I daresay, but I'll need a day to get it altered to fit me.'

There was a pause.

'I'm afraid,' said Angus slowly, 'that I can only give you money. I can't alter the time-schedule of the coach.'

'Nobody's asking you to keep the coach here for weeks,' said Maurice. 'All I need is a day.'

'I'm sorry,' said Angus.

Maurice stared at him in amazament.

'But . . . but you're not serious?'

'Why isn't he serious?' asked Mr Holt in his leisurely way. 'You may not be travelling on a strict schedule, but some of the other passengers are. Me, for one. Lord Lorrimer, for another. He told me he's got to be in Lisbon on the 25th. Well, so've I. So's Mr Zoller.'

'But it's absurd!' Maurice's voice rose. 'It's preposterous! Here I am, standing in a pair of pyjamas and a borrowed dressing gown and not another stitch to my name, and you expect me to rush out into those hot streets and chase wildly round outfitting myself completely in the space of a few hours!'

'I'm sorry,' said Angus again. 'It's bad luck and I'll do everything I can to help you, but I can't hold the coach.'

'You mean you won't,' said Maurice.

'I mean that I can't. I'm an employee of a Company which has guaranteed to get passengers to Lisbon on the 25th of this month. We – '

'Time-tables only operate,' said Maurice, 'if nothing comes up to cause a hold-up. Planes are late, trains are late, buses are late – and so the passengers don't arrive at the exact moment they've told their friends to expect them, and that's all there is to it. The passengers can't do anything about it. In the present case, a passenger loses his pants and the coach waits a day to give him a chance to buy a new pair; what's wrong with that?'

'It's hard on him, but he isn't the only one to be considered,' said Angus. 'If a passenger falls ill, we call a doctor, we engage a nurse, or we take him to hospital – but the coach goes on. If we schedule a time for departure and one of the passengers fails to turn up, we look for him and we make arrangements for him to be found and taken care of – but the coach goes on, as a train or a ship or a plane would go on. The Company has a time-table and short of accident – act of God – it keeps to it.'

'Rot,' said Maurice. 'All you have to do is use your own discretion. If you talked to the other passengers, you'd soon find that they – '

'I've been through to the Company's headquarters,' said Angus. 'The coach goes on.'

Maurice turned to appeal to Mr Holt.

'It's ludicrous!' he exclaimed. 'He can't do it. He's new to the job, and he's afraid to depart from his orders by a hair's-breadth. Tell him – '

'I guess you're getting a little mixed up,' Mr Holt told him calmly. 'You're mixing up inconvenience and emergency. You've suffered inconvenience, and we're all sorry – but we don't feel that this constitutes a real emergency.'

'That's because you're wearing your own pants,' said Maurice heatedly. 'It's all very well for you to array yourself on the Company's side – you've got something to array yourself in. I haven't.' He turned to Angus. 'If you think I'm going to leave this town with safety pins holding an ill-fitting suit in position,' he said, 'you'll have to think again. I'll put in a call to the Company on my own account.'

'Do that,' begged Mr Holt. 'And tell them that Lord Lorrimer and Mr Zoller and I – all valued customers – are anxious to get to Lisbon just when we said we would, and no later. Make your call, and then you'll feel a whole lot better and you'll place more reliance on Angus's word next time he reads out the rules. But I can tell you right now that what he says is correct: the coach goes on.'

Maurice stared from one to the other with a frown of anger; then, without another word, he turned and left them and went upstairs.

'Sorry about that,' said Angus, turning to Mr Holt. 'And . . . thanks.'

Mr Holt was still gazing thoughtfully after Maurice.

'I find that kind of interesting,' he said. 'Don't you?'

'I found it awkward, and I'm grateful to you for coming in on my side.'

'Oh . . . ' Mr Holt waved the thanks aside. 'A lot of things,' he observed, 'are happening on this trip. You don't know anybody around here that wants to make a few blots on your record with the Company?'

'It wouldn't matter much; I'm doing this trip and the return trip and that's all. Perhaps I'm a kind of Jonah, and with me aboard, nothing goes right. This seems to have been a chapter of accidents.'

'Accidents?'

'Incidents, then.'

'And all related, wouldn't you say?'

Angus looked at him. He liked the man, and trusted him; he would have liked very much to lay the sequence of events before him, not only to get his opinion, but also to clear his own thoughts. Theories and suspicions were jostling each other at the back of his mind, and he needed to disentangle them. Mr Holt would make a good listener and a sound counsellor – but he was a passenger and he had paid for a trouble-free trip.

He did not feel that the incidents had any connection with one another. He had believed Maurice Tarrant when he said that he had not tried the bolts of the garage door. Tarrant might have taken the despatch case; he had certainly tried to enter the garage – but it was impossible to imagine his going to the trouble of removing his own luggage. If he carried joking to those lengths, he would be certifiable, thought Angus – and there was nothing about the man that suggested a lack of intelligence. He was a nuisance, but he was not a fool.

For a moment, he thought that Mr Holt was going to enlarge upon his theory, but as he waited, the Admiral came down the stairs and spoke to Angus.

'Look here,' he said. 'I don't pretend to be one of those detective chaps who give away nothing for thirteen chapters and then give a long history of the case, but I do know this: something shady's going on. And if I'm not a detective, I'm something better: I'm a man of action.'

'Do we need action?' asked Mr Holt.

'It might come to that,' said the Admiral. 'Has it struck either of you that the thief might have got into the wrong room?'

'That had occurred to me,' said Mr Holt.

'That Zoller woman next door,' went on the Admiral, 'has a whole cartload of jewels, and doesn't mind telling you what they're worth. And that seems odd to me; women don't as a rule advertise the value of the trinkets they're carrying round. They – '

He paused. Angela was coming down the stairs; she joined the men and addressed Angus.

'Maurice is making a bit of trouble upstairs,' she said.

'What sort of trouble?' demanded the Admiral.

'He says it's absurd of Angus not to delay the coach for a day, and he's trying to get the others on his side.'

'Well, he won't get me,' stated the Admiral flatly. 'I'm sorry he's lost his luggage, but we can't sit here indefinitely, waiting for the thieves to return it.'

'He says he wants time to get some new clothes,' said Angela. 'He says he won't go on tomorrow; he's going to get through to the *Empress* headquarters and make a – a strong representation.'

'Ha,' snorted the Admiral. 'Well, I've made some strong representations m'self in m'time, and I'm going upstairs to make another one now. I'm not going to have my business run for me by a whippersnapper like Tarrant.'

He marched up the stairs, and Angela looked after him with a smile.

'I hoped he was going to say Damned Young Puppy,' she said.

'I'll go up and watch the fun,' said Mr Holt.

'You're worried,' she said to Angus, when they were alone. 'I'm puzzled.'

She waited, but he said no more. He wanted time to think. Suspicions, as vague as they were unlikely, were beginning to stir in the depths of his mind. Out of the confusion, certain facts were beginning to emerge; he might dismiss them for a time, but they returned again and again.

He heard Angela's voice.

'Do you think anyone's up to anything . . . anything serious?' she asked slowly.

'I wish I knew.' With an effort, he went on speaking lightly. 'Whatever it is, it can't be too serious. The whole thing seems to me to be on the practical joke level.'

'Are you going upstairs to see what's going on?'

'I know what's going on. If Tarrant succeeds in finding any supporters, and if they want me, they can come and look for me. And in the meantime' – he smiled – 'we're in Burgos and the sun is shining and there's a Cathedral you haven't seen. Will you have lunch with me?'

'Of course.'

But first, there were the police to see. There were questions to be answered, details to be given. It was well after noon when Angus was at last free to leave the building. He went to Angela's room and found her ready to go out. With her was Miss Seton, trim and cool in a linen suit. At Angus's heels came Mr Holt.

'I'm ready,' Miss Seton told him, and looked at Angus. 'Are you taking Angela sight-seeing?'

'If you're starting off with the Cathedral,' suggested Mr Holt, 'why don't we make four of us? I'll be the guide.'

'No; Angus will,' said Angela.

'No; I will,' said Mr Holt. 'I know this Cathedral like I know my own home.'

'It's a beautiful Cathedral,' said Miss Seton.

'It should be,' he said. 'It took three hundred years to build. Come on; let's go.' He ushered them out into the corridor. 'Wait till I tell you about Plateresque and Romanesque and Baroque and Rococo, not to mention Cimborium and retablos.'

'Goodness!' said Miss Seton.

'Tell me,' requested Mr Holt, on their way downstairs, 'how much you know about the Cid.'

'The – ?'

'You mean you want me to tell you?'

'No; wait. He's the national hero,' said Angela. 'Why bring him up now?'

Mr Holt led them out on to the street.

'Because this is his country. Ask Angus. No, don't ask Angus; let me tell you. This is the country of El Cid; you're walking this minute along roads that his horse's feet trod. You're in Burgos, and Burgos was once the capital of Castile, and Castile is the country of the Cid and – ' He stopped and stared. 'Well, well, well; if it isn't the Admiral and Mrs Denby-Warre.'

'Off to the Cathedral?' enquired the Admiral, lifting his Panama hat in deference to the ladies.

'Yes. Are you coming too?' Angela asked them.

'We shall look,' objected Mrs Denby-Warre, 'like a Conducted Tour.'

'And that,' said Mr Holt, 'is just what we are. You all are the tour, and I'm the conductor. This way, if you please.'

'Did you know,' asked the Admiral, falling into line, 'that this place Burgos is over 2780 feet above sea level?'

'I know,' said Mr Holt. 'If you'd stayed here in midwinter, you'd know too. If you – '

Once more he stopped. The whole party halted and stared in amazement at the extraordinary apparition coming towards them.

It was Maurice Tarrant. He was wearing tight black trousers and a short coat; on his head was a *Sevillano* hat. He looked very happy and very handsome.

'When in Rome,' he informed them airily, 'I invariably put on my toga.'

He posed obligingly while Angela and Miss Seton took snaps of him.

'Where were you all going?' he enquired. 'Not *sightseeing*?'

'Why not?' asked Mr Holt. 'There's a Cathedral over there and it's got inside it sixty tombs, forty-four altars and one hundred statues. We – '

'There's a little place over there,' said Maurice, 'where you can get a *vino fino* at about half a crown a quart.'

'I was going to say,' said Mr Holt, 'that we weren't, naturally, thinking of going sight-seeing on dry stomachs. Where did you say this place was?'

'Follow me,' said Maurice.

They followed him.

CHAPTER 8

ANGUS, with some difficulty, got Angela to himself for lunch. Thereafter, they were not likely to be disturbed, for between lunch and six o'clock the Spanish enjoyed a siesta, and most of the *Empress* passengers seemed to think the example good enough to follow. Only Miss Seton and Mr Holt were left seated together at a table in the deserted Square, intent and absorbed, and oblivious of Angela and Angus, who passed close by them.

'That looks hopeful,' commented Angus, when they had walked on a little way.

'Yes and no,' said Angela. 'I can see he's impressed, but I can't make her out. She's – she's not secretive, exactly, but she hasn't said much to anybody on the trip.'

'I think that she – like your father – has got something on her mind.'

'Do you know that, or are you just guessing?'

'I know that she got bad news over the phone the first night of the journey, but that's something I shouldn't tell you.'

She smiled.

'You take this job seriously, don't you?'

He looked surprised.

'I wouldn't have said so. Perhaps I see more in it than I did when old Sir Claud was writing it up in headlines. All I feel about it is that I'm being well paid and that the Company has high standards and that it's up to me to keep them high if I can – in return for the aforesaid pay packet. And that's why I'm sorry I've blotted the record.'

'Do you think Maurice is going to ring up London and argue about delaying the coach?'

'There's nothing to stop him. If he does, I imagine they'll advise him to stay behind when the coach leaves Burgos and offer to pay his expenses by air to allow him to catch us up.'

'Catch us up where?'

'Salamanca, I suppose – or further on, at the Portuguese border. But now that he's got his fancy dress on, he might decide to come on with us and get a new outfit in Lisbon. Are you tired?'

'No. Why?'

'Let's walk up the hill.'

'What's at the top?'

'Nothing much but the view. All that's left of the castle is a few stones.'

They walked slowly up and wandered, hand in hand, among the ruins.

'What happened here,' Angus asked her, 'in August 1254?'

'I've no idea, but it must be jolly hot here in August.' She sank on to a grass-grown mound and pulled him down beside her. 'What happened, anyway?'

'Edward I was brought here by his mother, to be married to Eleanor of Castile. She – '

'Angus, couldn't you enter for one of those quiz programmes and win an awful lot of money? You could choose English history and then – '

'Did you come up here to talk about quiz programmes?'

'I'm sorry. I'm truly sorry. Go on about Eleanor.'

'Will you please tell me why a bunch of people take the trouble and go to the expense of travelling all the way from London to Lisbon by road if they haven't the slightest intention of taking the smallest interest in anything they see on the way?'

'Darling, you wouldn't want us to go about in shorts and low-heeled shoes, carrying knapsacks and fat guide books and peering at things all the time?'

'All I'm waiting for is the first spark of intelligence in any one of the passengers.'

'But look how interested they were in Périgord.'

'That was gastronomic, not historical.'

'Well, what I really came up here for was to talk about

89

our future. Don't think I'm not interested in Edward and Eleanor; I couldn't be more so, but – '

'But you don't care if you never hear their names again?'

'All I was going to say was, now that you've got my father's approval – '

'I've got it?'

'Of course. Angus – '

'Well?'

'When we're married, will you tell our children that I pursued you relentlessly until you gave in and married me?'

He turned to smile at her.

'Yes. I shall tell them often, and at great length. I shall tell them that you had more honesty and more courage than any woman who ever lived, and that – '

He stopped. She was near, and she was as soft and as warm as the sunshine. The past was in the stones all round them. The future could be settled some other time – but this was the present and he must make the most of it.

Some time later, they saw two figures coming slowly up the hill, and identified them.

'Miss Seton and Holt,' said Angus. 'Perhaps she's brought him up here to talk about their future.'

'If so, they couldn't have chosen a better spot. Shall we let them have it?'

Miss Seton, however, seemed to have no desire to linger among the ruins. She and Mr Holt looked at the view, walked a little way and then came back and asked the others if they were going down.

'If so, let's go together,' she suggested.

The four walked down the hill, Angela and Miss Seton ahead, the two men following. Mr Holt seemed thoughtful, and said nothing for a time; then he put a question to Angus.

'All these what you call accidents,' he said. 'You got any theory about them?'

Angus hesitated.

'No,' he said at last. 'But I don't quite agree with what you said this morning about their being – about their having some connection with one another.'

'Well, I still think they're hooked up,' said Mr Holt. 'I told you it might be a joker, but I don't think so any more. Somebody means business. You remember the driver reported that someone had tried the bolts of the garage door? Did you follow that up and find out anything?'

Once more, Angus hesitated, and the other man gave a sigh.

'Oh, I know, I know,' he said. 'You're on the Company's payroll and your job is to keep passengers' minds on the scenery. And you'd like to discuss it with me, maybe, but you can't because you can't team up with passengers on business that strictly isn't theirs. That I see. So what it comes to, I just have to tell you what I think, while you keep what you think to yourself. That's how it goes, isn't it?'

'It sounds unfair, but that's how it has to be, I'm afraid. Do you know anything definite?'

'If I do, I'd like to look into it before committing myself. Swapping theories is one thing; undergoing cross-examination is quite a different thing. All I'm telling you is that in my view – and these glasses are good – I think everything that's happened has a tie-up; the incidents aren't isolated; they're following in logical sequence. And they've got one object in view.'

'Which is?'

'To delay the coach.'

There was a long pause. They were walking slowly, and both men were deep in thought.

'I think you must be wrong,' said Angus at last.

'Wrong? I don't think I'm wrong, but I can't prove anything – yet. I haven't got it figured out, but I'm working on it, and I'd get along faster if I could make anybody come out into the open and tell me what they know. But they won't.'

'They?'

'They. I know my grammar. When I say they, I mean the plural and not the singular. Nobody'll talk – and from now on, that includes me. But you know something? Tarrant won't ring up your headquarters and try to get the coach held up.'

'He's threatened to.'

'That was this morning. The day isn't over yet.'

The day was not over. When Angus got to his room, he found on his table a short message: would he go to the Admiral's room when it was convenient?

He went at once. Knocking, he heard the Admiral's voice and went in to find the old man standing at the window. On the table was the remains of a meal, and the Admiral jerked his head towards it.

'Had to eat something,' he said. 'Can't go till nearly midnight waiting for dinner.'

'You could always have dinner at eight if you wanted to, sir.'

'No, no, no. Got to keep in line. Don't want to travel and take all my home habits with me. All the same, it's a barbaric time, and it's playing hell with my inside. The food's enough to cope with on its own, but when you have to eat it at a time you'd normally be thinking of turning in . . . Oh well. Sit down, will you? Shan't keep you a minute.'

But as the older man showed no sign of seating himself, Angus remained on his feet and waited to hear why he had been summoned.

He had to wait some time. The Admiral walked up and down, stared out of the window, coughed nervously, gazed at the ornaments on a shelf and moved them a quarter of an inch to the right, coughed again and finally turned to face Angus.

'Just wanted to have a word with you about – er – something.'

'Yes, sir?'

'Yes. It . . . I hope I'm not keeping you from anything important?'

'Not at all.'

'Well.' The Admiral took a plunge. 'Ever heard of something called psychic phenomena?' he asked abruptly.

Angus, concealing his surprise, said that he had.

'Ah. Well, what I wanted to say was, my sister – Mrs Denby-Warre – is by way of being . . . er, psychic.'

Angus raised his eyebrows in polite attention, but said nothing.

'Wouldn't think it to look at her. I mean, people who go in for that sort of thing are usually crackpots, but she's got a very level head in other ways. But every now and then – not often; not more often, I'd say, than once or twice a year – she gets a . . . a sort of . . . of . . . *feeling*.'

The nervous cough came on once more, and the Admiral, recovering, gave Angus his fiercest quarter-deck look; he seemed to be searching for any signs of levity and was preparing to deal with them. Angus, however, spoke in a voice that betrayed nothing but interest.

'Really, sir?'

'Lot of people,' muttered the Admiral, 'don't believe in it.'

'I had a great-aunt,' said Angus, 'who had a gift of second sight. It was most extraordinary.'

How extraordinary, he did not feel it necessary to explain. Aunt Evelyn was dead and all those men she had seen chasing her had either given up the chase or were pursuing her round and round the heavenly mansions. How, he wondered, did it take Mrs Denby-Warre? She seemed an unlikely subject for visions.

'My sister didn't receive any manifestations – her word, not mine – until she was well over middle age, and I can tell you in confidence that I had my own ideas as to what was the matter with her. But I was wrong. One thing after another turned out just as she said it would, and in the end something happened that . . . well, it didn't reconcile me to this business of people seeing things, but it made me think. During the War, it was; not your war, naturally; one before. She said I was to take care, as she'd seen me in a bath chair. Thought she was making a joke, and thought no more about it, but damme if less than three days later, I wasn't in hospital with a bit of shell in m'leg. She came to see me, and the nurse trundled me out in one of those wheeled chairs, and when my sister saw me, she said, "What did I tell you?"'

He stopped, staring past Angus's shoulder at the nurse and the chair and the triumphant Mrs Denby-Warre. It was some time before he went on with his story.

'Ah,' he said at last, bringing his mind back with an effort. 'Well, this thing – this pre-vision or whatever you like to call it – came to her again last night.'

'She . . . saw something, sir?'

'She did. She saw the *Green Empress* in a ditch.'

'The coach?'

'This coach. I daresay they're all alike, but she says she's absolutely positive that it was this one. It was in a ditch. A Spanish ditch.'

'A – ?'

'That's what she said. It was a Spanish ditch. I asked her how she knew; a ditch, I said to her, is a trench of muddy water and you can't give it a nationality – but she said that it was this coach, and the ditch was in Spain. What's more, I was under the coach.'

'You were – '

'I was under the coach.'

A question hovered on Angus's lips, and he hesitated before

93

uttering it. Then the thought came to him that he had, after all, a right to know.

'Where,' he enquired, 'were the other passengers?'

'That's just the point. The odd part, I mean. They weren't there.'

'Not there?'

'No.' The Admiral coughed again in acute embarrassment. 'They weren't there.' A keen look satisfied him that he had Angus's grave attention, and he finished the story in a rush. 'The coach was empty. It was in the ditch – not in it, you understand; just partly in. And I was under the coach.'

There was a pause.

'Is she alarmed, sir?' asked Angus at last.

'Well, she doesn't like it. And so this morning, when she heard that Tarrant's luggage had been stolen, she was in favour of the day's delay. But then the question came up, and you vetoed it. So did I, at first – but she hadn't told me about her – her premonition or whatever you like to call it. So we talked it over, and I said I'd explain the circumstances to you and tell you that if there's going to be a vote on waiting a day, or going on, we're in favour of waiting.'

Angus frowned.

'But I don't quite see, sir,' he pointed out, 'how Mrs Denby-Warre can be certain that the delay would prevent the – the catastrophe. If she doesn't know exactly when it's to happen, mightn't it be a possibility that the day's delay is going to be the very factor that causes it?'

The Admiral stared at him, a baffled expression on his face. 'Hadn't thought of that,' he mumbled.

'I think we shall be going on, sir – but perhaps that point of view, if you put it before Mrs Denby-Warre, would reassure her.'

'Might do.'

'How do you feel about it, sir?'

'Me?'

'You were the –'

'Oh, yes, yes, yes. See what you mean. Well, m'own feeling is that I don't particularly want to end up in a Spanish ditch, but if that's where they've put my number, that's where I'll find it, and going on, or not going on, won't make much odds.'

'I don't think, sir, that even if Tarrant gets in touch with London, they'll authorise a delay.'

'That's what I thought. That's what I said. But she insisted on your being told about the – the dream, or whatever you like to call it. She thought you ought to know. Don't run away with the idea that I care one way or the other. I came to tell you this solely on my sister's behalf.'

'I think that we shall be going on, sir.'

'Very well. I shall tell her.'

They went out of the door together. The Admiral marched towards his sister's room, and Angus walked thoughtfully back to his own.

He was still pondering when he went down a little later to spend some time with the manager, talking over the events of the night. Half his mind was on the interview, but the other half was on what Mr Holt had said about the attempts to delay the coach. Tarrant, this morning, had been anxious to keep the coach back for a day. Now Mrs Denby-Warre seemed equally anxious to provide an excuse for delaying the *Empress*. Mrs Denby-Warre . . . or the Admiral.

When he returned to his room, it was to find on his table another message. This was more cryptic than the last. On a plain sheet of paper was written, in block capitals, a few words:

CUPBOARD IN CORRIDOR OUTSIDE TARRANT'S ROOM.

He left his room at once and went to the floor above. Walking along the corridor towards the cupboard, he was in no doubt about what he was going to find. Opening the cupboard, he saw without surprise what he had expected to see.

On the wide shelves were Maurice Tarrant's two suitcases, his clothes and his shoes.

CHAPTER 9

ANGUS did not at once tell Tarrant of the recovery of the luggage. He wanted time to think, time to reassess the situation.

He went thoughtfully back to his room, but before he reached it, he found that he had changed his opinion about the unlikelihood of Tarrant's having removed his own luggage. The facts seemed to fall into place, and he viewed them with a new clarity. A thief might have decided to take the suitcases as well as their contents, but he would hardly have paused to pick up articles of little or no value that had been unpacked and were lying about the room. The intruder – if it was an intruder – had left nothing, not even the clothes hanging in the wardrobe. And being left with nothing had given Maurice Tarrant as valid an excuse as Mrs Denby-Warre or the Admiral for suggesting a readjustment of the *Empress* time-table. They had wanted to hold the coach back – why, he could not begin to guess.

And now somebody had found the luggage and removed at least one excuse for delay.

He stared at the paper and the writing. It gave no clue. The paper was one of the sheets of writing paper provided in every desk in every bedroom. One set of paper had printed headings and another – intended, presumably, as second sheets – was plain. Every passenger and every member of the staff could use the paper; the block capitals gave no clue to the writer's own hand.

He folded the paper, slipped it into his pocket and went to Maurice's room. He had to knock several times before making himself heard over the strains of the Spanish song that Maurice was singing in his bath. At last there was a pause, and Angus heard a shout.

'*Quien es?*'

'It's Graham.'

'Come in, my dear fellow, come in.'

Angus went in. Across the room was the open door of the bathroom; beyond it, almost lost in steam, was the figure of Maurice, draped in an enormous towel.

'Sit down,' he called. 'I'll be out in a minute. Been having a siesta. Wonderful way to live, this. At home, think what we'd be doing at seven in the evening: planning some sort of dinner and perhaps going on to a theatre or a film and getting out well before midnight with not much to do but go home to bed. But here? At midnight, they're just getting up from dinner.' He walked into the bedroom. 'One seems to get a longer day in this country, and that of course means a longer life. Why are you standing up?'

'I'm not staying. I came to tell you that your luggage has been found.'

Sheer surprise made Maurice's mouth open, and he stared at Angus for a few moments during which the latter registered the fact that this was the first time anything had silenced Mr Tarrant.

'*Found?*'

'Yes.'

The obvious question did not follow; Maurice did not seem curious to know where his property had been recovered. Angus took the paper from his pocket and held it out.

Maurice took it, and as he looked at the words on it, the bewilderment left his face and gave way to a grin of enjoyment.

'Detective stuff,' he said slowly. 'Well, well, well.' He looked at Angus. 'Any idea who wrote this?'

'None. Have you?'

'I could make two guesses, and one of them would be right.'

'Why don't you want to know where the stuff was found?'

'You're not' – there was reproach in the tone – 'you're surely not going to accuse me of knowing where it was, are you?'

'There's not much point in making accusations. I don't feel that anybody but you could have done it, but I can't for the life of me think why you'd play a fool trick of that kind. To delay the coach, perhaps – but why?'

'Look, my dear Angus.' Maurice's expression was that of a patient man explaining something to an obstinate one. 'You seem to have put me down as one of those characters who go around giving the international police endless trouble. Why would I want to hold the coach back? I've got an appointment with a firm in Lisbon and I've got to keep it. I don't want to, but I'll soon be scraping the bottom of the financial barrel, and my mother's got the idea that it's time I put a bit back into the till. When I suggested that the coach ought to wait a day while I bought myself some clothes, I felt I wasn't being unreasonable, but you can't surely be seriously suggesting that I would spend the hours of dawn lugging my own luggage here and there and hiding it under the floorboards merely in order to push the *Empress* off schedule?'

'I don't know, and to be frank, I don't care,' said Angus. 'I wish I could work it all out, but I can't. I'm no detective. I'm a courier. My job is to get this coach to Lisbon on time, and I'd like to tell you, now that we're on the subject, that if you've any other delaying tactics in view, you can forget them. Unless somebody wrecks the bus, we're going on.'

'You have an admirable sense of duty.' Maurice made the

compliment sound almost sincere. 'But do try to get it into your head, my dear fellow, that I've just as much reason as anybody else for wanting to get to Lisbon. And now let's order a couple of drinks.'

'I can't stop, thanks. I've got to let the manager know what's happened.'

'Couldn't we just bring the luggage in here and say it was miraculously restored?'

'It was miraculously restored,' commented Angus dryly, 'but we won't say so. Let's go and get it.'

They brought the things from the cupboard and put them in the bedroom.

'Can I have that paper back?' asked Angus.

'Of course.' Maurice handed it to him. 'What are you going to tell everybody?' he asked curiously.

'I shall tell the staff that you've been the victim of a practical joke. It won't do anything to increase their respect for the English, but it's better than getting the servants involved in more questioning.'

'And the passengers?'

'They can work it out for themselves.'

He left Maurice, but he did not go back to his own room. When he had spoken to the manager, he made his way to the room occupied by Mr Holt.

When admitted, he went straight to the point. Laying the paper before him, he put a question.

'Do you know anything about that?'

Before replying Mr Holt offered Angus a cigarette, took one himself and waited until they were alight.

'Sit down,' he invited. 'No, not there; the other chair's more your size.' He indicated a comfortable chair near the long windows which led on to the balcony, pushed another chair close to it, and seated himself. 'Pleasant out here, isn't it? Last time I was here, it was so hot that I had them push my bed out on to this kind of verandah, and I was the only one who got a cool night's sleep. Now. What's on your mind?'

'Do you know anything about what's written on that piece of paper?'

'If I did, I wouldn't want to tell you anything about it.' Mr Holt was leaning back in his chair; as always, he was completely relaxed. 'What I know is my own affair – but what you get to know is the business of the *Green Empress* Company. Isn't that correct?'

'Yes, but – '

'And now that you know where the luggage is, you can let the whole thing drop.'

'I told them down in the office that it was a practical joke.'

'Good boy. And now tell me why you wanted to get me mixed up in it.'

'I thought, when you were talking to me today – first in the morning, and later when I met you with Miss Seton – that you knew more than you were telling me.'

'I still do. And you know what I'd do in your place? I'd let everybody have their fun, and I wouldn't take a mite of notice – until, of course, it looked like interfering with the Company's business; then you put a stop to it, as you did this morning when Tarrant was giving trouble. All you have to do is mind your own business, which is the Company's business. You don't have to lose sleep trying to figure out whether you're carrying normal passengers or chimpanzees. You didn't choose them, and just so long as they get in and out of the coach when they're supposed to, and follow the programme, you don't have to worry about how they amuse themselves at the night stops. The less you see, the less you know. The less you know, the less you have to report to headquarters. Stick to the main issues; that's sound advice.'

There was a pause. Then Angus smiled.

'Yes,' he said. 'I think it's sound advice. 'Thank you. The only thing is – '

'Is what?'

'It all makes me feel a fool. I don't particularly mind looking a fool if I've done something foolish, but I would have liked to be able to reach a few satisfactory solutions in my own mind.'

'Me too. If it's any comfort to you, I don't know much, and all of it is fact. When I get to theorising, none of it makes much sense. So let's forget it. Tell me, are you taking Miss Lovely out tonight?'

'No. She's dining with her father and Yule.'

'Are congratulations in order, or am I merely imagining that one and one are about to make one?'

Angus rose and stood smiling down at the other man.

'Things are . . . in train,' he said.

'Then congratulations are in order and I won't make any obvious cracks about in coach rather than in train. Are you – '

He stopped as a knock came on the door. Mr Holt called a

careless *Adelante*, and Angus saw that he was expecting one of the servants to enter – but when the door opened, it was Miss Seton who was standing on the threshold. Angus caught an expression of surprise on Mr Holt's face, and then it had given way to a smile of pleasure and he was hurrying forward to welcome her.

'Come in, come in, come in. It's nice of you to call. I was just giving Angus some good advice. I've told him to keep his eyes on the road and not let the passengers distract him.'

'Not even when they lose their luggage?'

'Not even when they find it again.'

She looked from one man to the other.

'The luggage has been found?'

'It has,' said Mr Holt. 'Angus decided it must be a practical joker, and so he went a-looking. He found Tarrant's grips in a cupboard and he restored them to the owner.'

It was some moments before Miss Seton spoke, and Angus, to his surprise, found that the colour had slowly receded from her cheeks.

'I'm so glad,' she said at last.

'You're glad, I'm glad, he's glad – and perhaps Tarrant's glad too; who knows? I was on the point of suggesting to Angus, when you came in, that we might go out to dinner to celebrate. Will you join us?'

'If you'll forgive me,' said Angus, before she could speak, 'I think I'll go out on my own and do something I haven't had a chance to do for some time – go round the little out-of-the-way *tascas* talking to the natives and brushing up the lower brackets of my Spanish. I'd ask you to join me, but some of the places aren't exactly what Miss Seton – '

'Here's how we'll do it,' suggested Mr Holt. 'If Miss Seton will dine with me, we'll fix a meeting place and Angus can take us round some of these dives after dinner . . . How'd that work out?'

It was agreed that they would meet after dinner. Angus, after fixing a time and a place, went out and left the other two alone. As he walked down the corridor, a servant stopped him with a message to the effect that Mr Zoller would like to see him. Before the last words were spoken, Mr Zoller's great bulk appeared round a corner and he hailed Angus in his guttural voice.

'Ah – so! It is Mr Graham. I have been looking for you. Can you speak with me?'

'Certainly. Would you like to come to my room?'

'No, no, no, thank you. The matter is short. All I ask is will you permit that my wife and I shall come downstairs to this floor and so make a change to a room with a balcony?'

'I think it could be arranged,' said Angus. 'But . . . hasn't your present room a balcony?'

'Yes, there is one – but it is very narrow, and it has no cover, no roof. Down here, there are not perhaps balconies but verandahs, and my wife wants to have one. I have been asking, and I find that there is an empty room along here, next to the American's.'

'There's a double room between Mr Holt's and Miss Seton's; is that the one you want?'

'That is the one. It is big, the balcony is big, there is more air. Can you order that our things are changed from one room to the other?'

'Of course. I'll do it now.'

'As a madderfact,' confided Mr Zoller, 'my wife is nervous since Mr Tarrant's luggage was taken. Yes, yes, I know that it has come back; just now, when I spoke to the manager about the room, he told me that all it was is a practical joke, but even so, she doesn't care to stay up there. So I said to her that I would see if an empty room was downstairs.'

'I'll go and make the arrangements.'

Angus went to do so, wondering why there should be a faint feeling of distrust in his mind. The request was a simple one, and it was easy to believe that Mrs Zoller wished to remove herself and her jewels from a room next to that in which a robbery had taken place. It sounded reasonable, but behind Mr Zoller's apparent frankness, Angus had sensed something that made him vaguely uneasy.

He remembered Mr Holt's advice; easy advice to follow, since it fell into line with his own inclinations. He wanted to do the job well, but he did not feel capable of solving the small mysteries that had irritated him in the course of the journey. Maurice Tarrant was irresponsible, Mr Holt enigmatic, Mr Zoller secretive. Miss Seton showed little interest in the loss of the luggage, and paled on learning of its recovery. The Admiral was apprehensive; his sister was having visions. Things disappeared, things reappeared. Mr Holt was right: the thing to do was to get on with the job and leave the side-issues to settle themselves.

He longed, suddenly, for a sight of Angela. He wondered whether she would be in her room or whether she would already have gone out. He was about to put the matter to the test, when he almost ran into the Admiral, who was coming out of his room.

'Ah. Funny thing, I was just thinking about you,' said the old man. 'Can you spare a moment?'

Angus would have liked to say that he could not, but the Admiral was already ushering him into the room. Closing the door, he took a few paces to and fro with his hands clasped behind his back, apparently preparing his address; then he came to a halt before Angus.

'Tell you what,' he said gruffly. 'I've heard that that fellow's luggage has been found, and I've come to the conclusion that there's somebody among us who's either trying to be funny, or not trying to be funny. Either way, you've got to find out who he is and throw him out before he goes too far.'

'I'm afraid, sir, that I can't – '

'You can't throw him out on suspicion; admitted. But you can keep your eyes open, and next time he tries anything, you can catch him at it. You can keep a look-out. And so can I – and that's what I'm going to do. From now on, if I see anybody doing anything that looks like being another of those blasted silly practical jokes, I shan't stop to ask why he's doing it; I shall act. I'm not dead yet, by a long chalk. I don't suppose I'm up to anything strenuous, but I was a sound boxer in my time and I daresay I could still land a punch or two. So if you get a signal from me, you'll know that I've caught somebody napping, and unless you're close enough to deal with the matter, I shall deal with it myself. Have I made myself clear?'

'Yes, sir.' Angus hesitated. 'But may I point out that so far, nothing that has happened has been very serious, and – '

'Look here,' broke in the Admiral. 'There are ten of us on this trip. Our safety is in your hands, and in the driver's. Barring road accidents, we hope to arrive in Lisbon in good shape. There's no harm in jokes, even in practical jokes – though I think they're the resort of the mentally deficient – in the proper place. But among strangers, on a long cross-country journey, practical jokes are definitely out of place. Soon, this fellow'll be tinkering with the engine of the coach, or interfering with one of the women, making them look foolish, or something of that kind. I'm not going to expose my sister to a risk like that. The thing has gone far enough, and from now on, I'm going to be on the look-out. That's all I had to say.'

'Thank you, sir. I'll be on the look-out, too.'

'I don't like naming names, but my money's on Tarrant.'

'Why would he take his own luggage?'

'To put us off the scent. You mark my words: it's that fellow. He's an exhibitionist, and as a rule chaps like that aren't burdened with a sense of proportion. I don't know what he's up to, but I know what he's going to get next time he tries to let off one of his squibs. Well, don't let me keep you. What time do we set off tomorrow?'

'About eleven, sir. Eleven fifteen, to be exact.'

'Where are we bound? Oh, Salamanca.'

'Yes. We go to Valladolid and – '

'Where?'

'Valladolid. Then south-west to Zamora and – '

'Can't understand this zigzagging, myself. Why can't we set a straight course and stick to it? We've been tacking ever since we left Calais.'

'You'd miss some interesting places, sir,' he explained. 'There'll be time to do a bit of sight-seeing at Valladolid. Columbus died there and – '

'That all we're going there for?'

'Well, we – '

' 'Tisn't where he died that's interesting; it's what he did while he was alive.'

'It's also the birthplace of Torquemada, and – '

'Torquemada?' The Admiral's brows came down. 'Torque-*ma*-da?'

'Yes, sir. He – '

'Do you mean the Spanish Inquisition Torquemada?'

'Yes, sir. He – '

'Do you mean to tell me' – the Admiral's voice rose from a menacing growl to a clap of thunder – 'do you mean to stand there and tell me that we're all to be herded tomorrow to a place in which the most diabolical fiend in all history was born? Do you? Do you?'

'I – '

'Do you mean to say that you're going to expound, to-morrow, on that devil and all his works? Do you? Because if you are, you can address your information to those who want to hear it. I don't. Do you think I left a pleasant home and a beautiful garden in order to come and gloat over a period of history that cries stinking shame to the very name of religion? Do you? Will you for God's sake explain to me why decent people from decent parish churches all over England come to the Continent and stand gaping at all this blood-and-thunder Christianity? I don't want to see any more gory representations of Christ on the Cross. I'm as good a Christian as the next man, but I can say m'prayers and ask for salvation without having my stomach upset. Let me tell you – '

He stopped abruptly. The door had opened and Mrs Denby-Warre entered hastily and closed the door firmly behind her.

'Rodney! Whatever are you thinking about?' she asked in horror. 'I could hear you shouting from the next room!'

The Admiral's sentiments were still being expressed, but in lower tones, and she frowned in displeasure.

'You're not, I hope, arguing about religion?'

'This fellow,' said the Admiral, 'started me off by telling me that tomorrow's the day for refreshing our memories of the Spanish Inquisition. So I told him to address the rest of the class and leave me out.'

'Why can't you be reasonable? The Spanish Inquisition took place and – '

' – and it was a blot on civilisation and we ought to be scrubbing it out, not bringing parties along to pay the old fiend the compliment of remembering where he was born.'

'Why should you blame Mr Graham?'

'Who's blaming him? I didn't say a word about him. I merely said – '

'Yes, yes. I warned you, Rodney, not to wait too long for dinner. I told you to order some food early, and – '

'I'd give my soul,' said the Admiral yearningly, 'for a good pair of kippers.'

Mrs Denby-Warre gave him a despairing gaze, and then turned to Angus.

'I wonder, Mr Graham, whether you could kindly order something brought upstairs now?'

'Something plain, for God's sake,' implored the Admiral. 'You can keep your pie-ella and your squids in ink gravy.

Just send me up a lamb chop, if they've got one, and some nice little new potatoes' – his voice had a yearning sound – 'and some green peas fresh from the garden, or some tender green beans and a little bowl of junket with some fresh strawberries and a blob of cream on top and a bit of decent English Cheddar . . . '

There was silence. The room, with its rich hangings and huge bed and stiff painted wooden chairs, receded and gave way to cream-washed walls, a plain, trim bed and a mahogany chest of drawers. Outside, the brown Spanish landscape seemed to have melted into the soft green tones of England. A faint smell of lavender hung in the air, and Mrs Denby-Warre and Angus, withdrawing silently, left the Admiral alone to enjoy it.

CHAPTER 10

ANGUS lost Miss Seton and Mr Holt at the third *tasca*. For the rest of the evening he wandered alone, thinking of Angela, of her father, of the future. Walking homeward at last, he reviewed the events of the past few days and tried to find running through them the thread which – according to Mr Holt – connected them. He arrived at the door of the hotel without any theories which he felt would stand up to investigation.

The next morning was brilliant with sunshine, and he threw off all thoughts that could cloud the day. Everything in Spain, he thought gratefully, splashing in his bath, was golden. Its sherry, its sun, its soil, its villages perched on hills. And today the *Empress* would plunge deep into the Moorish past, to the Spain of Arab dominion that had left its mark for ever on Spanish life and mood and music.

Today the *Empress* would go through Zamora, once a frontier town. Towelling vigorously, he recalled that King Ferdinand I had rebuilt it – but who had razed it to the ground? Who? Reaching for a shirt, he found the answer: it was a gentleman by the name of Al Maneour.

He broke into a loud rendering of Swanee River, the upward octaves a little shaky. Then he sang it through again to a topical lyric.

> 'Back, back again to Moor-*ish batt*-les,
> Back, back we go;
> Back, long before they beat *Bo-ab-dil*,
> Back to the old Arab foe.'

Pleased with his versatility, he brushed his hair and called permission for his breakfast to enter. He drew a chair up to the table and looked at the tray with growing appetite. *Churros* to be dunked in coffee. Excellent *churros*, excellent coffee – but perhaps not enough *churros*; ring for more. Why couldn't one get them at home ? Perhaps, to get their full flavour, they would have to be imported with the wizened old men who fried them, and the little dark boys who carried them through the streets, piping hot, in a cloth-covered basket. *Churros*; here they came, second lot, every bit as good as the first, and Hsst! wait a minute, perhaps you'd better bring me another lot of coffee to wash them down.

Breakfast over, he went out with the intention of knocking loud and long upon Angela's door. If she was not ready, he would wait for her, and then they would go down and pay a morning visit to Ferdy.

He walked along the gallery towards her room. Glancing over the wooden railing to the hall below, he saw something that brought him to a halt.

In the hall, neatly aligned, were six suitcases: the Zollers'.

He stood still for a moment. There was no reason why the luggage should not be there. It was early for the cases to have been brought downstairs, but perhaps the Zollers had risen early and were now out, taking a last look at Burgos. All the same . . .

He walked to the head of the stairs and saw that Mr Zoller had entered the hall. He looked up and saw Angus, and the latter walked downstairs and joined him.

'Good morning. I have been looking for you,' said Mr Zoller. 'I am so sorry to tell you that we have been called away.'

'I don't quite understand. Do you mean you're not going to Lisbon ?'

'Oh, we are going to Lisbon; yes, oh yes. But I have had a message – an urgent message, you know – that I am wanted there at once. I have been sent for already. I have to go at once, and I told the manager to arrange for me to have a car. He said that he must first ask you, but I said to him – you will excuse me for this ? – I said that I had asked you and you had given permission. It is a pity we have to go – we are so sorry.'

There seemed nothing to say. Worse, there seemed nothing to do. Mr Zoller had ordered his car, had his luggage brought down and now was standing, coat over arm, hat in hand, ready to leave.

Questions sprang to Angus's lips, but there seemed no point in uttering them. He was bound to accept Mr Zoller's statement. There was nothing he could do but see him off.

Mrs Zoller came downstairs, her informal clothes discarded; she wore a linen suit and her usual array of jewels. She held a plump hand out to Angus.

'We are so sorry to go,' she said. 'But it is important – my husband has told you already ?'

'Yes.'

'Will you please say to the others that we are sorry not to tell them goodbye ? We shall see everybody in Lisbon.'

Angus looked at Mr Zoller.

'There's just one thing puzzling me,' he said. 'No messages are ever taken direct to passengers, and I – '

'It was extraordinary, you know.' Mr Zoller's small, bright eyes were fixed unblinkingly on Angus's. 'I was coming down the corridor, and here is this telegram for me. The man did not want to give it up, but I said that you would not mind and perhaps you would be sleeping. I did not think that you would object. And now' – he held out a hand – 'goodbye, Mr Graham. If you are going to be on an *Empress* to return to England, I hope that we shall see you. Goodbye.'

'Goodbye, goodbye,' called Mrs Zoller on her way to the car.

Angus walked to the top of the steps and watched them as they settled themselves. Mr Zoller handed his wife in, waited to count the pieces of luggage and tip the boys, and then got into the car beside his wife. He raised a hand in farewell and then they had gone.

He turned and walked into the office. It did not take long to confirm what he knew already: no message had come to the hotel since the day before. There was no possibility that Mr Zoller had met and bribed a member of the staff. Breakfast had been taken to his room at an early hour and the maid had remained to help Mrs Zoller with her packing. Neither Mr nor Mrs Zoller had left their room until they went downstairs to the car.

Angus walked thoughtfully upstairs and entered the room

they had occupied. Maids were at work clearing the beds, and he walked out on to the wide balcony and stood trying to guess what had made husband and wife depart so abruptly.

He waited for ideas, and none came. If anybody needed a detective's stooge, he thought morosely, he could give an entirely natural performance.

The sun slanted on to the balcony. On one side of the low dividing wall was the balcony of Miss Seton's room, on the other, Mr Holt's. No sound came from Miss Seton's side, but the clink of crockery suggested that Mr Holt was having his coffee. For a moment, Angus thought of going in to see him. Here was another inexplicable incident; perhaps Mr Holt would see the connecting thread running through this one too.

Instead of going to Mr Holt's room, he went to Angela's. She was not there, and he went in search of her and found her at last in the small, wall-enclosed garden.

He took her wrists, holding her prisoner, and bent and put his lips on hers. The garden was cool and deserted and peaceful, and the worry in his mind died away, leaving him calm and at ease.

She drew away at last, took a deep breath and looked at him.

'Your breakfast must have agreed with you,' she said. 'Tell me what it was, and I'll have it on your plate every morning when we're married.'

He looked down at her, his expression sober.

'I love you,' he said. 'I don't care whether it's madness or not, or whether it's taking advantage of your kindness of heart or not. I love you. I don't know anything about Canada, but if you're there, it'll be all right. If we're poor, we're poor. If I'm taking you from a gold-plated past to a tin-plated future, I'll try to make it up to you. I'll work for you. I'll love you all my life. I'll take care of you. I'll be a good father to our children, and to the end of my days I'll remember that it was your courage that brought us together. When can we be married?'

'When you start moving, you move fast,' she commented, and quoted softly:

' "*How is it you're so early of late? You used to be behind before, but now you're first, at last.*" '

'When will you marry me?'
'Now. There's just one thing – '
'Well?'

'You won't get any silly ideas about leaving me behind while you make a home for me over there? I couldn't bear it if you went off and – '

He frowned.

'That reminds me.'

'Of what?'

'The Zollers. They went off.'

'Went off where?'

'They hired a car and left for Lisbon. He said he'd been sent for in a hurry. He said something about an urgent message, but it was a lie. I checked. I came down just in time to see them going off. He'd made all the arrangements, and there was nothing for me to do but stand there like a fool and wave them goodbye.'

'They didn't make any complaints?'

'None. He even went so far as to say he'd be making the return trip in an *Empress*, but . . . '

'But what?'

'I don't know. I feel that if only I could see it, this would be tied up with all the other things that have happened on the trip. Holt says there's a connecting link.'

She led him to a bench and drew him down beside her.

'Sort it out,' she suggested. 'Begin at the beginning and then perhaps it'll clear itself up as you talk. My father says that articulation leads to clarification. Say it all, just as though I weren't a passenger.'

'You won't discuss it with any of the others?'

'Cut my throat.'

'Well, it's all completely unrelated, as far as I can see, but I'm coming round to Holt's idea. There must be some sort of connection; it can't just be a series of misadventures.'

'Where do you think it began?'

'The night Miss Seton got a telephone message. Not night; early morning, about two. I took her down to the phone and waited for her while she took the call. It was bad news, but I didn't know what kind.'

'Is that why she turned so quiet?'

'Yes. Then somebody tried to get into the garage; you and the Admiral came along just as Ferdy was telling me about it. Then Tarrant tried to climb through the garage window.'

'*Maurice* did?'

'Yes. Ferdy tried to catch him, but all he succeeded in doing was hitting him on the wrist with a torch – and that's how I found out it was Tarrant: I saw the mark on his wrist.'

'Then?'

'Then the despatch case disappeared – and was pushed into your father's room. Then Tarrant's luggage went. Somebody put a note on my table – unsigned – telling me where to find it. It's hopeless to try to get anything out of Tarrant, but Holt seems to know something, and won't tell me what it is, because I'd have to report it to the Company. He said, in effect, that I wasn't responsible for anything that took place outside my sphere of duty. I felt that he was right, and I made up my mind not to worry about it – and then Mr Zoller talked to me about changing his room, and this morning made up a lying excuse and left. It can't just be one damned thing after another. They're not isolated incidents; they're connected. They're related.'

There was silence.

'It's easy,' said Angela slowly at last, 'to let one's imagination run away. Mine did at the beginning of the trip, when I couldn't discover what was making my father so depressed. I found that I was beginning to . . . well, to work myself up. I had to shake myself out of it and tell myself that if I could do anything, he'd tell me – and until he said something, it was useless to imagine this and that. And I think the same goes for you. Don't try to fit the pieces together. Do as Mr Holt said: don't make them your business unless or until you have to.'

He frowned.

'Did you really worry seriously about your father?'

'Yes. He was – and still is – completely unlike himself. As a rule, he's – he's amusing, and interesting, and tremendous fun to be with. But now . . . he's gone off somewhere by himself. He broods nearly all the time. He dreams, and he loses the thread of what he's saying. I wouldn't mind that, if he didn't look so unhappy. If you look at him when he doesn't know you're looking, you see that he's . . . '

'How long has he been like this?'

'Since he came home from Greece. He was there for a month – not on a one-day thing like this present job, but a long and I think much more important mission.'

'Couldn't he be suffering from strain?'

'I thought so, but he seemed perfectly all right for a time – and then just before we came on this trip, he seemed to get miserable again. And it's such a shame, because this holiday has been planned for ages, and we were going to have fun.'

He looked at her worried face and bent to kiss her.

'You see?' she said. 'We're in the same boat; we can see that something's wrong, but we can't work out quite what it is. And so if we stop worrying, things will sort themselves out. Won't they?'

He grinned.

'I can sit back and leave everything to the Admiral. He told me he was certain that Tarrant was behind it all, and he's lying in wait for him.' He rose. 'Come and see Ferdy; after that, I've got to inform headquarters that two of the passengers have left the coach.'

'Must you tell them?'

'Yes. Orders. They must be tired of chalking up all the details.'

'Will they hold it against you?'

'That won't matter much. I hope they won't hold it against Wax Sealing for recommending me.'

They walked slowly across the garden, and a small, smiling boy threw open a door to admit them to the house. Angus paused to look down at him and to say a few friendly words.

'It was your father's car, I hear, that Señor Zoller hired?'

'Yes, Señor. It is a good car, a new car. And my father is a good driver. Tonight they will reach Caceres; tomorrow, my father said, he will get the Señor to Algeciras.'

For a moment Angus stared at him, and then he walked on beside Angela. She glanced up at him uneasily.

'Why did they say they were going to Lisbon if they were going to Algeciras?' she asked.

He had no answer to give her. He had not the remotest idea why they had gone to Algeciras — or even why they had gone at all.

CHAPTER 11

THE coach, without the Zollers, looked strangely empty.

Angus, after the first half hour of the run, suggested a change of places: Mrs Denby-Warre moved across to sit behind Angela, and the Admiral moved into her vacant seat behind Maurice Tarrant. The seating had now a more balanced appearance, but the minds of the passengers remained on the Zollers.

'Odd sort of pair,' said the Admiral, to nobody in particular. 'Wonder how he made his money?'

'He didn't make it,' answered Maurice. 'Other people made it for him. It's the sort of thing we'd all like, but very few of us manage to bring it off. Zoller gets on to the track of someone who's got a scheme but hasn't the money to launch it. He doesn't advance him the capital; he simply buys the idea and it always turns out to be a gold mine.'

'How do you know?' asked Miss Seton.

'Oh, just by talking to him,' said Maurice airily. 'I dined with them last night and they both opened up surprisingly. Zoller told me that his original capital was nothing more than an infallible sense of what was going to pay off. He said that he doesn't have to think about money matters; he merely feels. Knowledge is no good unless you've got the instinct; he just has to shut his eyes and let his instinct guide him.'

'Rather him than me,' grunted the Admiral. 'When I close m'eyes, I don't want to see money.'

'I do,' said Maurice. 'Zoller told me that everything he bought paid off. All his businesses thrived. Throve? Thrived. It was reassuring to have all that money next door to me. I missed them last night.'

'Last night?' Miss Seton's tone was surprised. 'I thought Mr Graham said they didn't leave until this morning.'

'They didn't,' said Angus, 'but they asked me if they could change their room. They went down last night to the empty room between yours and Mr Holt's.'

'The . . .' Her eyes were fixed on Angus, and he saw their expression slowly changing. 'The room next to mine?'

'Yes.'

'You mean that they were there last night?'

'Surely not?' put in Mr Holt. 'Miss Seton and I came in fairly early and there wasn't a sound and there wasn't a light.'

'They were there,' said Angus. 'They were probably asleep when you came in. And they were up and away very early this morning, so you probably didn't hear them.'

'What was their hurry?' asked the Admiral. 'I understood that they didn't have to be in Lisbon until the 25th.'

Angus hesitated. Mr Zoller's business was his own. But he had said that he was returning to England on an *Empress* and it was not unlikely that some of those now in the coach would be with him and they would learn that he had not been called to Lisbon.

'They didn't go to Lisbon,' he said.

'Back to England?' enquired the Admiral.

'No. They went to Algeciras.'

'Algeciras?' Miss Seton's voice was so amazed that Angus turned to look at her. She was staring at him, her face pale and drawn. 'Are you quite certain they went to Algeciras?'

'They hired a car and they'll get there tomorrow,' said Angus.

'Did he . . . Was it a telegram?' she asked slowly.

'I'm afraid I don't know,' said Angus. 'Nothing came through me.'

'But I thought,' said Mr Holt, 'that all messages had to go through you. The office would never let me claim my stuff until it had been handed over to you.'

'Mr Zoller said that he didn't want to disturb me.'

'I see.' Mr Holt stared past Angus at a point on the landscape and spoke thoughtfully. 'So Zoller changed his room, spent the night in the one between Miss Seton's and mine, got up early and departed in a hurry for Algeciras. Right?'

The words were quiet, and only Miss Seton and Angus were listening; the attention of the others had left the Zollers. But when Angus nodded in reply to Mr Holt's question, he saw a look pass between him and Miss Seton, and saw the blank dismay in her eyes. Then it was gone, and she appeared to give her attention to what the others were saying.

They were nearing Valladolid, and Maurice mentioned Don Quixote.

'Who?' asked the Admiral.

'Don Quixote. You've heard of Don Quixote?' said Maurice in amazement.

'Never in the whole of m'life,' said the Admiral aggressively.

'Of course you have, Rodney,' said his sister with a touch of irritation. 'Rodney, do *think*!'

'Windmills,' prompted Maurice. 'Damsels in distress. Sancho Panza.'

'If you're talking about Don Quicksote, of course I know,' said the Admiral angrily. 'Do you refer to Paris as Paree, or to Florence as Firenze? No. So why give Don Quicksote a fancy pronunciation? And why bring him up at all?'

'Because the first part of the book was written by Cervantes at Valladolid,' said Maurice. 'The house is a State monument. I'll take you round,' he offered. 'Lots to see.

Columbus died there, Philip II was born there and Cervantes lived there. What more could any city ask? Only one thing, and now it's going to get it: Maurice Tarrant lunched there.' He looked at Angus. 'Let's have drinks now, to celebrate.'

If anybody had asked the Admiral to look at the sights of the city before lunch, he might have agreed; as the suggestion was made after he had eaten *gazpacho*, *tortilla* and *ternera con tocino*, no spark of enthusiasm could be raised in him. Brushing aside Angus's suggestion that he should enjoy the siesta hours in the cool, quiet lounge kept expressly for *Empress* passengers, he went out and walked to the square in which the *Empress* was parked. Climbing in, he followed the example of Ferdy in the driver's seat: he pushed his chair back to its lowest angle, lay back, closed his eyes and added baritone snores to Ferdy's tenor ones.

He was still asleep when the passengers re-embarked.

'Don't disturb him,' said Angela softly.

'He could have seen so much!' mourned Mrs Denby-Warre. 'He could have learned so much. Surely one can stay awake in surroundings like these?'

The Admiral, however, stayed asleep for the next fifty miles, and awakened in a mood unconducive to the appreciation of scenery.

'Yes, yes, yes,' he said sullenly to his sister, as she handed him a map. 'I know where we are. We're on our way to Salamanca, and we could have gone there in a straight line, instead of trapesing round the country.'

He rose with the intention of following Angus back to the observation compartment. The coach gave a slight lurch, and he clutched the back of Miss Seton's seat to steady himself.

'What's that river?' he asked her.

'The Douro.'

'Can't be,' said the Admiral. 'The Douro's in Portugal.'

'Only the business end of it,' pointed out Maurice.

The Admiral stared out at the river, his expression changing slowly to one of reverence.

'The Douro!' he said slowly. 'Port!'

' 'Sright,' said Maurice.

'Port!' intoned the Admiral. He sent an angry glance round the coach. 'Why can't we follow the river into Portugal, instead of wasting time at a lot of other places? We'd see the vine terraces, and those boats, forget what they call 'em, that carry the wine down to Oporto.'

'That's scheduled for the return journey, sir,' said Angus.

'Couldn't we stop and take a look at the river?' asked the Admiral.

'We could, sir. I'll talk to the driver. We cross it when we leave Zamora, and he could stop after that.'

The place Ferdy chose was a pleasant stretch of road that afforded a backward view of Zamora. The passengers got out of the coach and walked a little way, picking out landmarks; only the Admiral kept his gaze on the water and let his imagination rove over its lower reaches and saw the wine on its way to Oporto. Port. Rich, rare port. He had a couple of bottles of '27 he'd been keeping for – for what? He'd better drink it soon, or somebody'd drink it at his funeral. Port . . .

He marched along the bank, and Angus watched him with a smile. Mrs Denby-Warre came to stand beside him, and spoke hopefully.

'I really think,' she said, 'that he's beginning to take an interest in the scenery at last.'

'I'm sure he is.'

'He told you' – she turned to look up at him – 'about my – shall we call it dream?'

'Yes. I hope you're not worrying about it?'

'It's no use worrying, you know. One accepts. One resigns oneself. One waits.'

'Not waits, I hope, to see the Admiral under the coach?' he said gently.

'Waits to see what fate has in store. I saw an empty coach: two seats are now empty. Hasn't that struck you as extraordinary?'

'To tell you the truth – '

He never told her the truth. A shout had come from the direction of some trees overhanging the river and Angus, swinging round, saw the Admiral running, plunging through hanging branches, lumbering awkwardly but valiantly in the direction of the clump of trees that were closest to the water. He vanished behind foliage, reappeared, vanished again – but before disappearing, he had turned and yelled loudly to Angus.

'Got him! Come on!'

Angus began to run – not fast, but steadily. If he went too hard, he reminded himself, cursing, his knee would let him down. He took a short cut down the bank, making for the trees behind which the Admiral had disappeared. Mrs Denby-

Warre's anxious cries fell behind him, thinned and died away.

He was going downhill, down to the trees, guided now by a loud and triumphant shout from the Admiral. Before he had taken many more steps, he heard the crash of branches. The broad back of the Admiral appeared, and Angus saw that he was striving desperately to keep his balance. Arms flailing, he staggered backward a few more paces and then, before Angus could reach him, fell heavily and rolled down the bank.

Angus, making a lightning calculation, chose a place at which he could arrest the Admiral's downward progress, and with a lunge, reached the spot, braced himself and waited. A rough estimate of the old man's weight made him feel almost certain that far from stopping the rapidly-descending form, he would merely check it momentarily and then go down with it – down into the brown water.

He heard the Admiral's hoarse breathing, felt a rush of loose pebbles – and then the weight was on him and he felt himself being borne downward. He dug his heels into the earth, clutched desperately at the undergrowth, slithered a few more yards and finally stopped at the water's very edge.

The next moment, he had got to his feet and was bending over the Admiral's heaving frame.

'Are you all right, sir?'

'I . . . ' The old man fought for breath. 'I . . . saw . . . '

'Who, sir?'

The Admiral shook his head.

'Didn't see . . . didn't get . . . proper look. Saw the devil st-stealing away and . . . and made a grab and . . . '

'You're hurt,' said Angus.

'No. Yes. My arm, damn it.'

'Let me see, sir.'

Mud-streaked, his face scratched, his clothes torn, the Admiral struggled, with Angus's help, to a sitting position. Voices were heard coming nearer, and a heavy pounding told Angus that Ferdy was on the way.

'Didn't see the f-fellow,' the Admiral brought out. 'Saw him moving off through the trees . . . made a dive . . . got a hold . . . lost it. The devil was going to . . . '

His voice, to Angus's dismay, faltered and died. His eyes closed. He sank back, and Ferdy hurtled down the bank in time to aid Angus in lowering the old man gently to the ground.

'What happened, sir?' he panted.

Angus hesitated. The others were near. Suspicion was one thing, accusation another. If it could be proved that the Admiral had seen Maurice Tarrant . . . but he had not been able to identify the man. Nor had he stated what had aroused his suspicions.

'I don't know, Ferdy,' he replied.

'His arm, sir,' said Ferdy, at the end of a gentle examination.

'Yes. We'll have to get him back to the coach.'

There were willing helpers. Maurice Tarrant and Lord Lorrimer, who had come down together, were fetching water. Miss Seton was getting a coat to put over the Admiral. Ferdy was loosening his clothes. Kneeling on the ground and supporting her brother's head was Mrs Denby-Warre, pale as death, but admirably calm. Issuing quiet orders, she made her brother comfortable and signed for silence as his eyes opened.

'Perfectly all right,' he muttered, looking at the anxious faces round him. 'No need to fuss.'

'Your arm is hurt, dear,' said his sister.

'Nothing to speak of.' Struggling, the Admiral sat up and was helped to his feet by Ferdy and Angus. 'Perfectly all right. Nothing to worry about.'

The words were steady, but it was clear to the others that he was badly shaken. Leaning on Ferdy's broad shoulder, supported on his other side by Lord Lorrimer, he began a slow ascent of the bank. The others fell in behind, and the melancholy procession made its way back to the coach.

Angus let them go. He wanted a moment to himself. He wanted to be alone, to think – and to look. The Admiral had seen something up there among the trees. Somebody had been creeping away. Creeping away from what?

It was not long before he found out. It was a crude enough trap – a hastily-arranged, loose arrangement of hanging branches looped in such a way that, if unseen by somebody coming towards it, it would trip him and send him into the river below. It was not a long drop; it would not be a dangerous fall: a stumble, a wetting and perhaps some minor injuries.

The Admiral had seen it – and he had seen somebody creeping away from it. He had given chase, but he had found that his speed and strength were not what they had once been. He had fallen, and now he was on his way to the coach between the twin supports of Ferdy and Lord Lorrimer, his arm sprained, or worse, and his whole frame severely shaken.

Angus tore the branches of the clumsy trap apart, and prepared to follow the others. At his feet he could see signs of the struggle that had taken place when the Admiral had so nearly caught his man. A stronger hold, a firmer grasp, and he would have had him. But the hold had slipped and the man had got away.

And then he saw on the ground something else.

He stared incredulously at it for some moments, and then stooped and picked it up. He held the tiny scrap of material in his hand, and as he gazed at it, anger, black and shaking, misted his sight and made his hands shake.

He thrust the piece of cloth into his pocket, and after waiting a moment to regain control of himself, walked swiftly after the others. Angela turned and waited for him, and as he drew near, came to meet him and stared in surprise at his expression.

'Angus, what's the matter ?'

'Nothing.'

'You're . . . you look terribly white.'

'I'm all right. We'll . . . we'll talk about it later.'

She walked by his side, saying nothing, and he was grateful to her; he needed a little time to force himself back to coolness. He brought his mind, with an effort, back to the Admiral, and fell into step beside Mrs Denby-Warre.

'We'll go on to Salamanca,' he told her quietly. 'It's only a matter of forty miles. They'll get us a doctor and we'll be able to make the Admiral comfortable in his own room.'

She nodded. She was the picture of composure, and he began to feel a new respect for her.

'Why did he shout and begin to run ?' she asked.

'I daresay he'll tell us when he's feeling a little better.'

They made the Admiral comfortable in the two seats vacated by the Zollers. He lay back on one; the other, turned about, made a support for his legs. Ferdy drove at speed, but with a skill that roused Angus's admiration. The Admiral said little, but he said it with force.

'Not going to be left behind in this Salamanca place,' he told Angus. 'Don't you think it for a moment.'

'I don't think there's any need for that, sir.'

'Nothing the matter with m'arm. Slight sprain, that's all.

Don't want any foreigners messing about with it. Get a decent doctor at Lisbon.'

They reached Salamanca, and Angus remembered that he had stayed, not so long ago, in a large room in a house situated in a street that led off the famous *Plaza Mayor*. It had been a noisy room; for the few hours he had spent in it each night, he had been unable to sleep – but his days had been filled with interest; he had seen everything that was to be seen inside famous buildings, and then he had wandered through the streets of the city, falling hour by hour more deeply under the spell of its beauty. Salamanca, with its golden stones . . .

And he was here once more, but there was nothing more in his mind than anxiety about one man and a longing to get his hands on another and reduce, once and for all, his nuisance value. Gloom filled him as he remembered that he had considered himself, on the whole, a fairly good judge of men. He had believed himself capable of making a reasonably good estimate of character – but in this case he had been, he acknowledged, miles off the mark. He had been fooled. Worse, he had been treated like a backward boy, and he had fallen an easy victim to smooth talk. Perhaps it was salutary to learn that he could be as big a fool as anybody else.

But now the evidence was in his pocket. The evidence; the proof.

Ferdy brought the coach to a stop before a beautiful building decorated with an ancient coat of arms. The *Green Empress* staff, dark, serious, polite, showed genuine concern for the Admiral's mishap. He was helped upstairs to his room and made comfortable, and a doctor was sent for.

'How long do we stay here?' the Admiral wanted to know.

'Only one night, sir. We leave in the morning.'

'And I leave with you,' stated the Admiral flatly.

'Of course, my dear,' said his sister soothingly. 'Did anybody suggest your staying behind?'

'They'd better not,' grunted the Admiral.

The doctor, arriving with commendable speed, proved to be a tall, grave, middle-aged man who said little, but handled the patient with expert gentleness. Angus was present as interpreter, and Mrs Denby-Warre stood quietly by, ready to assist if necessary.

'Don't know what he's diagnosed,' said the Admiral at the end of the examination, 'but you can tell him from me that I'm all right and that I'm going on to Lisbon in the morning.' He glared at the doctor and addressed him in a loud, clear tone, enunciating each syllable with emphasis. 'Arm all right,' he informed him. 'Arm O.K. Speak French? *Bras bong; rien* the matter with it whatsoever.'

The doctor bowed, and in rapid Spanish informed Angus that the arm was sprained, but not badly; the gentleman should, in his opinion, rest for twenty-four hours; at his age, and with his build, it was not wise to ignore the effect of shock. But if, as was to be seen, it proved too difficult to persuade him to go to bed, no great harm would be done if he insisted upon continuing the journey.

'What's he say?' demanded the Admiral suspiciously.

'He says that if you feel equal to going on, you can do so, sir.'

'Said that all along,' stated the Admiral. 'Got sense, this chap; not like some foreigners. Tell him I said so, and thank him and get rid of him.'

With the departure, some time later, of the doctor, Angus prepared to withdraw. The injured arm was in a sling, and the Admiral's sister had cleaned him up and restored him to something like his normal neatness. He thanked her gruffly and grinned up at Angus.

'Can't shake her,' he said. 'Solid as a rock in emergencies. You've got to say that for English women; got their heads screwed on.'

Mrs Denby-Warre smiled down at him.

'It wasn't altogether a surprise to me,' she reminded him. 'I knew. I felt inside here' – she indicated, with the utmost delicacy, her bosom – 'I felt that something was going to happen to you. And my dream, if we may call it a dream, came true.'

'True?' The Admiral stared at her in surprise. 'You said I was going to be under the coach. Don't remember being under the coach, unless somebody put me there when I was out for those few minutes.'

'But the coach was empty – you remember, Rodney? The coach was empty. I had seen it empty in my dream, and –'

'But you'd seen it in a ditch.'

'But don't you see? The ditch was the river! The coach was empty' – her voice was rising sharply – 'the coach was empty and the . . . the ditch was there and you were all m-muddy and –'

'Here, steady on, old girl,' admonished the Admiral.

'I saw it all! When I heard you shout, I t-told myself that it had c-come at last. You were in danger, and there was the empty c-coach, the empty coach, the empty – '

'Good God, her needle's stuck!' The Admiral was on his feet, whiter than his recent experiences had succeeded in making him. 'Here, Graham, get her into a chair.'

' – empty coach,' sang Mrs Denby-Warre, on a high and wavering note. 'Ha ha ha! There you were, going down, ha ha ha, down towards the ditch ·and there was the empty coach, the empty coach, the – '

'Quick! Don't just stand there!' roared the Admiral at Angus. 'Do something, can't you? Slap her face! Get some water! Get her head between her knees! Get – '

'Ha ha ha ha ha!' shrieked Mrs Denby-Warre. 'Oh, Rodney, it was so terrible, so t-terrible! There was the empty coach and the empty coach and the – '

'What the hell are you doing?' the Admiral bellowed at Angus. 'Who wants water? Take your hands off her, d'you hear? Go and fetch that blasted doctor – go on. Go ON, d'you hear me? Go and GET him. Go and GET him. GO AND GET HIM! FETCH HIM BACK!'

Angus fetched him back.

CHAPTER 12

FOR the next few hours, Angus was too fully occupied with practical details to be able to spare any time for thought. He had to reorganise the travel arrangements of two of his passengers: Mrs Denby-Warre, in bed in a darkened room, had recovered her self-control, but there was no question of her travelling for the next few days, and the Admiral, who had been unwilling to stay on his account, had no hesitation in deciding to remain behind with his sister. He issued contradictory orders for the comfort of the patient, barred visitors from the sickroom and growled when anybody mentioned his own accident.

'I'm all right,' he insisted, looking fiercely at Angus. 'You see that my sister's looked after, that's all. You could start by showing them how to make a decent cup of tea. The last lot they sent up was made of straw.'

'The doctor didn't advise tea, sir, and – '

'When a woman feels she needs a good cup of tea, she should have one. And don't let anybody barge in on any of those so-called sickroom visits. She doesn't want to see them. She doesn't want to see anybody – except m'self, naturally. But you'd better go in now'n then to see that orders are being carried out. And don't you leave this place without making fool-proof arrangements for getting us out of it. I can't talk this blasted tongue and I don't want to, so just you see that everything's written down for them so's they know what they're about when the coach has left. Four days: no more. I want to leave here, with my sister, five days from now. Two days in bed, one day up, one day about; that's all she needs. See to it.'

Seeing to it, Angus found no leisure and no opportunity to deal with other matters. When at last he had arranged every detail to the Admiral's satisfaction, and read out, in his presence, a lengthy list of instructions to the staff, he found that he was tired, hungry and longing for Angela's company.

On the way to her room, he met her on the way to his. They stopped and for a few moments studied one another.

'I feel,' said Angus slowly, 'as though I hadn't seen you for years.'

She put out a hand and touched his cheek.

'You look tired. Have the patients been troublesome ?'

'Only one of them. Can't we go out somewhere and have dinner ?'

'That's what I was coming to ask you.'

Facing her across a table less than half an hour later, he felt grateful for the way in which she steered their conversation clear of all matters relating to the journey. He was, she reminded him, off duty; this was their evening and not Sir Claud's.

Angus was content to put tomorrow's problems aside. Once, when she referred glancingly to the fact that when the coach left Salamanca, there would be only six passengers aboard, he was on the point of telling her to subtract one more – and then changed his mind. He would tell her to-morrow; tonight was for other things.

'What are you dreaming about ?' she asked, after watching him during a spell of silence.

'You. And the soothing effect you've had on me. I came out tonight feeling a bit on edge.'

> ' "Like the notes of a fiddle, she sweetly, sweetly
> Raises our spirits and calms our fears," '

she quoted. 'I can't claim all the credit; you've eaten two helpings of shellfish and practically an entire chicken, so that's had a lot to do with raising your spirits sweetly, sweetly. Angus – '

'Well?'

'Couldn't we live in Spain? We've been so happy here.'

'I don't see why we shouldn't. There must be a number of castles to let.'

'No castles. I want a white house with a shadowed patio and a river near by where all the village women wash the clothes. Can you play the guitar?'

'I could try.'

'After dinner, we could sit in the soft air in the patio, and you could strum – '

' – a soft air?'

'Darling' – she looked at him with awe – 'that was almost funny. Did you mean it?'

'It just slipped out. Would you prefer Spain to Canada?'

'It sounds a bit unpatriotic, in a way, but you must admit that there are still parts of Canada where they hand you a pickaxe and tell you to hack down the virgin forest and throw yourself up a log cabin.'

'There are parts of Spain in which you have to guide your plough in and out of rocks and boulders.'

'Could you make a living in Spain?'

'If I couldn't, you could, judging from the effect you have on the male population. Drink your wine. I want to get you away from all these people, get you to myself, get you into my arms.'

She put her elbows on the table and stared at him thoughtfully.

'Something's worrying you.'

'Yes.'

'You don't really mind what the Company thinks, do you?'

'I'm sorry for poor old Sir Claud. He's not going to like this wholesale dispersal of his customers.'

'But there's something more than that on your mind – isn't there?'

'Yes. But I don't want to talk about it until tomorrow.'

'Nor do I. It's about Maurice Tarrant, isn't it?'

He hesitated.

'Yes.'

'Well, don't be too hard on him.' She frowned. 'Haven't you noticed something?'

'Yes.' His eyes, with a grateful look in them, went to the narrow band round her hair – the small scarf, gay with printed fans. 'But this isn't an anniversary?'

'I wore it because I thought you'd feel better if I reminded you that I love you with all my heart.'

'I . . . Angela, my darling . . . '

'Stay just the way you are until you've paid the bill and got me into a less populous spot. You love me?'

'I love you.'

He got back to the hotel calm and refreshed, and realised that it was for this that she had sought him out and spent the evening with him. She loved him – but she loved him unselfishly. The word helpmeet, which he had considered out of circulation, came into his mind and brought with it a new warmth and trust.

When he went to say good night to Ferdy, he found him gloomy. Four from ten, he told Angus dejectedly, made four empty places, and there had never, in all his experience, been a single empty seat on a *Green Empress*. It was not, he acknowledged, Angus's fault; if a lady had to have hysterics, then she had to – but for a driver with a clean sheet, this series of upsets was the worst possible misfortune.

'I've brought you bad luck, Ferdy, and I'm sorry. But . . . there won't be six in the morning. There'll only be five.'

Ferdy stared at him, his mouth agape.

'*Five*, sir? You mean somebody else has gone and dropped out?'

'Somebody else is going to be dropped out – by me. And if you don't mind, that's all I can tell you at the moment. Tomorrow, I'll give you the whole story.'

'You don't have to, sir,' said Ferdy, his countenance brightening. 'I wish we'd got rid of that young spark before ever we crossed the Channel. With him gone, I'll feel a lot better. You've cheered me up, sir.'

Angus slept uneasily, and woke early. Having bathed and dressed, his first visit was to the Admiral. He found him in a loose, much-darned dressing gown, drinking his morning tea.

'Just been in to see my sister,' he announced, as Angus

entered. 'She's had a good night, and she's feeling more like herself.'

'I'm glad, sir. And you?'

'Me? I'm fine. There's another *Empress* coming in this evening, I understand?'

'Yes, sir. She'll be in at about five. She's on her way home from Seville.'

'Might get a chat with one or two of her passengers. I shan't feel so marooned. What time are you off?'

'Not until midday, sir; it's not a long run.'

'Where do you make for?'

'We lunch at Ciudad Rodrigo; after that we cross into Portugal and stay the night near Guarda.'

'Well, we shan't be long after you, I hope. Come in and say goodbye before you go. And if it isn't too early in the morning, I'd like to offer m'congratulations. Had a word with Lord Lorrimer last night when you were out with the daughter, and I hear it's pretty well fixed up.'

'I hope it will be soon, sir.'

'She's a nice-looking girl. If I were forty years younger, I'd be envying you. Take my advice: wherever you settle, get yourselves a garden. Teaches you planning and teaches you patience. If you'd like to ring for another cup, there's plenty of tea in the pot.'

'No, thank you, sir. I've rather a lot to do.'

'Well, look in before you go.'

Angus went out and closed the door. And then he was on his way to another room, thankful that at last there was to be an end to conjecture and to suspense. Proof was proof, and he had it in his pocket.

He knocked, and was asked to enter. As he went in, he took the small piece of cloth from his pocket – and then he walked up to the man seated in his shirtsleeves on the edge of the bed, and held out his hand, with the incriminating shred of material on the palm.

'You lost that?' he asked quietly.

Silence fell and held for a long moment. Mr Holt stared down at the evidence, and then his eyes came up to meet those of Angus. Finding in them nothing but hard enquiry, he shook his head slowly from side to side.

'Oh my, oh my,' he intoned. 'Now look what we've got ourselves into.'

'It's yours?'

'Of course. You know it's mine.' His tone was resigned. 'That's where exhibitionism gets you: if I hadn't worn those noisy checks, you might have placed the blame where the blame's due.'

'The Admiral saw you – and tried to catch you.'

'He did. Does that mean I was doing any harm?'

Angus stared down at him.

'Look, Mr Holt,' he said slowly, 'I don't understand what you've been up to, but this I know: we've all had enough. I wouldn't have said that you were a man who'd spend his time playing elementary jokes like these. I'd put it down to Tarrant, who's the type you could believe capable of any kind of idiocy. But you . . . I'd got you in a totally different category.'

'And I hope you'll keep me there.' Mr Holt rose, stepped close to Angus and tapped him on the chest. 'Me, I'm as sick of the whole thing as you are.'

'Are you denying that you're the man the Admiral caught?'

'Tried to catch. No, I'm not denying it. I was there, and he saw me – but I wasn't there to set that tomfool trap. I was there to take it down.'

'Who set it?'

'Tarrant.'

'For whom?'

There was a pause. Mr Holt walked to a cupboard, opened it and took out his jacket. Getting into it, he turned to face Angus.

'In the melodramas,' he said, 'this is the place where the actor chews his lips, turns aside and mutters: "Alas, the secret is not mine to di-vulge." Well, I can say that too. But there's a time for not talking and there's a time for talking – and this is the time for spilling some information. But before I spill it, I'm going along to ask permission.' He took Angus's arm. 'You come with me, young man, and we'll go where the whole thing started.'

He led Angus out and along the corridor. He knocked on a door, and Angus did not need to ask whose it was.

'Come in,' called Miss Seton.

They went in. She looked at Angus, at first in surprise and then, as she read the expression on the faces of the two men, with a kind of weary resignation.

'Oh,' was all she said.

Mr Holt closed the door.

'May we sit down?' he asked. 'Or would it be better to say it all standing?'

'We'll stand,' said Miss Seton. 'How much does he know?'

'He knows nothing beyond the fact that there's been a lot of monkey business,' said Mr Holt. 'He knows that Tarrant rigged up a trip-trap and that the Admiral saw it and saw what he thought was the guy who rigged it. He knows that the piece of shirt the Admiral got hold of is mine. He came in, all six feet two of him, with the plain intention of lifting me into the air and throwing me out of the window. In self-defence, I told him I'd talk – if you'd give me permission to talk.'

He paused. Miss Seton's face was white, and she had an exhausted look.

'So I suppose we tell him?' she said slowly.

'It would have been wise,' said Mr Holt gently, 'to have told him right at the start. But you didn't tell him, and now he's had all he can take. And so, to tell you God's truth, have I.' He led her to a chair and placed her in it. 'Sit down there and tell it in your own words. Go ahead.'

Miss Seton sat down. In a few moments, she raised her eyes and looked at Angus.

'You know the beginning,' she said.

He hesitated.

'The telephone call?'

'Yes. It was from my mother. When she told me why she had telephoned, I . . . at first, I couldn't believe it. It wasn't until she read me the letter, word by word, that I knew it must be true.'

'What did she tell you?' asked Angus gently.

'A letter had come from my sister.'

'From Rosamond?'

'Yes. I'm glad you knew her. I'm glad you saw her, because it makes it easier for you to understand how I felt when I heard the news.' She paused. 'You know that she had been filming in Italy?'

'You told me.'

'She was going on to South America to make another film . . . we thought. But she wrote to me just before she sailed; she didn't know that by the time the letter reached England, I would have left – would be on my way to meet her. My mother recognised her writing and opened the letter. She . . . she . . .'

There was silence. Miss Seton seemed unable to go on.

'What was in the letter?' asked Angus after a time.

'She wrote that she was going to South America, but she
. . . she wasn't going to make a film. At Lisbon, she was
meeting somebody who was joining the ship and going to
South America with her. They were going to wait there until
he got his divorce – and then they were going to be married.'

'Marry . . . Who is he?' asked Angus.

'Lord Lorrimer.'

There was a long, tense pause. Angus, his mind in a daze,
could only stare at her.

'Lord Lorrimer!' he brought out at last, in stupefied tones.

'Yes.' Her voice broke. 'A man old enough to be her father.
A man who is a father, with children not much younger than
herself. A man already middle-aged, a man who's had his life.
And she's . . . she's twenty-eight.'

'Where . . . where did they – '

'They met in Italy. She was in Brindisi. He was on his way
home from Greece. They met – and fell in love. He stayed on,
and for a time they both forgot . . . everything. She had never
been in love before, and she said that it was . . . it was over-
whelming. They agreed that he was to go home for the
marriage of his son, but he said that he would join her again in
Italy and go to South America with her. Then, at the last
moment, she . . . she refused. She sent him away, and he went
back to England and she tried to forget him. But she couldn't.
It might have been easier if he hadn't told her that he had to
go to Lisbon to attend an international conference; when she
found that he would be there on the very day her ship called
there, she . . . it seemed to her to be fate. She wrote to him just
before sailing, telling him she had changed her mind. Before
the ship sailed, she felt that she couldn't go without writing to
me and asking me to break the news to my mother. And my
mother opened the letter. And . . . you know the rest. I . . . '

Tears coursed down her cheeks; her voice died away and
she dabbed angrily at her eyes. While he waited for her to
continue, Angus fought to shake his mind clear of the fog that
was beginning to shroud it. Lord Lorrimer – and Rosamond
Blake. The story was still to emerge, but one fact he had
already grasped: Angela was to learn that her father was
running away, leaving his wife, leaving his home and his
children. Her father was on his way to Lisbon – but he would
not be returning.

He heard Miss Seton's voice, and forced his mind back to what she was saying.

'When I heard the news, the only thing I could think of – after the first shock – was . . . was what an appalling waste it was. For both of them. The letter she wrote wasn't the letter of a happy woman going to join the man she loved. She loved him – but she knew what she was taking him away from. She knew that she was breaking up a marriage that had lasted for more than twenty-five years. She knew that they would both be buying their happiness at a terrible cost. She knew it – but she was going to meet him. They' – she paused to steady her voice, and then went on more quietly – 'they were coming nearer together, and once they met, I felt that it would be too late for anybody to do anything – but when I went back to my room after hearing the news, I lay wondering why something couldn't be done to – to give them both time to think, time to reconsider, time . . . just time. I felt that if only the coach hadn't been scheduled to get to Lisbon on that date, Rosamond wouldn't have changed her mind. And it seemed to me that if only the coach could be delayed – just for a few hours – those few hours would be enough. He wouldn't be able to meet the ship. She would arrive – and he wouldn't be there. Time, time, time. That's all that was needed. Time. And so – I made up my mind that I must do something to keep the coach back.'

'It wasn't' – Mr Holt's quiet voice took up the tale – 'it wasn't a very good idea. But people act strangely under shock – as the Admiral's sister showed us yesterday. Miss Seton was acting under shock when she decided to go downstairs, get into the garage and remove a few vital parts from the engine of the *Empress*.'

'I didn't know whether it would hold us up or not,' said Miss Seton, 'but I was desperate to try anything – anything. When I found the door locked, and started to come back to my room, I was beginning to realise that I'd acted stupidly. The only thing was – '

'The only thing was that Tarrant had seen her,' said Mr Holt. 'He'd heard you both go down to the phone. He heard Miss Seton go down again – and he followed her. He saw her trying to get into the garage, and naturally he asked her what it was all about. And most unfortunately, she – '

'I didn't tell him,' said Miss Seton. 'But he got it out of me, bit by bit. When I sit here and say this to you, I can't believe that I could have been so crazy – but try to put your mind back and imagine how I was feeling. If I'd been myself, I would have realised that the only thing was to get away from Maurice at once and let him surmise anything he could. But I thought I could keep my head and tell him some kind of story that would satisfy him. I couldn't. When I got back to my room, I was thinking clearly, but it was too late.'

'And from then on,' said Mr Holt, 'Tarrant has been taking the initiative. He wasn't interested in the actors, but the situation seemed to offer an opportunity for some fun – and so he took it. His first attempt at delaying tactics wasn't a success; all he got was a crack on the wrist.'

'When did Miss Seton tell you?' asked Angus.

'She didn't tell me. I told her. I saw her with Yule's despatch case.'

'When the case disappeared,' said Miss Seton, 'I knew that it must be another attempt on Maurice's part to cause a delay. He thought – I suppose we all thought – that the papers in it were important. But they weren't.'

'So when you offered to help me look for the case,' Angus asked her, 'you knew he'd taken it?'

'I was pretty sure. I knew he must have put it into one of the lockers – his own, probably. And he had. You remember that it was raining when we got out of the coach? He put his coat on his arm, and as he went past Lionel Yule's seat, he picked up the case and hid it under his coat – and then it was easy to stoop down and put it into his locker. I opened it and saw the case – and Mr Holt saw it too. When I said nothing, he knew that something was going on between Maurice and myself.'

'And so I went first to Tarrant,' said Mr Holt. 'He sent me to Miss Seton. And she told me the story, and that's why I was looking out for signs of trouble yesterday. I knew that Tarrant would try something, in spite of having been told by Miss Seton – and by me, more forcibly – to lay off. It didn't take long to find the branches all hooked up. He was with Lord Lorrimer, walking with him up to the spot where the accident was to take place. I was unhooking the branches when I saw the Admiral on his way over – at speed. He'd given the old Cub call and was a-coming. He grabbed my shirt and he got two-green-and-red checks and a button – and then he lost his balance and went down. I could have said something to you then, but I hadn't been able to persuade Miss Seton to let me talk. I wanted her to tell you, or to let me tell you what was going on, before there was real trouble. There's no real harm in Tarrant, but you know how it is: these juvenile types start something for fun, and then they go on with it for more fun, and next thing you know, they've taken it up in earnest. You watch two little boys playing, the same thing happens: they start out dealing each other playful taps, and suddenly they're rolling in the mud trying to batter one another to pulp. Tarrant's trouble is just that: he doesn't know when to stop.'

'How,' asked Angus, 'did you know where he'd hidden his luggage?'

'That wasn't difficult. We're not dealing with a clever man; just a silly one. Everything he did, he did crudely. He didn't stop to think out anything; his plans were as childish as the way he put them into effect. I knew he must have put his grips into the first place he could find that they'd fit into – and it had to be the cupboard outside his room, where the servants wouldn't think of looking for a passenger's baggage. I was pretty sure you'd know I'd written the note telling you where the stuff was – but at that time, Miss Seton was still holding out against talking.'

'I didn't want to tell you,' Miss Seton told Angus, 'for several reasons. My first instinct had been to tell you what Rosamond was going to do – but I didn't tell you that night, and after that it was too late, because it became clear that you were going to be closely connected with Lord Lorrimer. And once the delaying attempts began, I couldn't say anything to you because you were on the side of the Company.'

'And she also knew,' said Mr Holt, 'that Angela Clunes was going to be hurt badly when she learned the truth about her father, and she thought that if she told you, it would put you in a difficult position. And now she's told you, and you're in it. But we're all in it: Lord Lorrimer, and Miss Seton, and Tarrant and you and I. The Admiral and his sister got mixed up in it, and so did the Zollers.'

Angus stared at him in surprise.

'How do the Zollers come into it?' he saked.

'If Miss Seton's guess is correct – and I think it is – then Zoller is the guy who bought the author who wrote the play that's being made into the film that Rosamond Blake has been offered so much to appear in. The chain of events can't just be coincidence. Figure it out for yourself: I go up to Tarrant's room, the room next to the Zollers', and I tell him that I don't know what he's doing, but he's got to stop doing it. He didn't give much away, but he said two things, and he said them clearly enough to be heard through those thin walls: one was Rosamond Blake's name, and the other was the advice to go and ask Miss Seton for the whole story. I don't suppose Zoller started out listening, but when he heard Rosamond Blake's name, his ears must have taken up a receptive attitude. So first of all, he asked Tarrant to dine with him, and after giving out a lot of phoney information about himself, proceeds to extract a few facts from Tarrant. He learns enough to know that if he can hear what goes on when I talk to Miss Seton, he'll learn a whole lot more. So he changes his room and comes down to the one between Miss Seton's and mine. He and his wife retire early and put out the lights, and when I come in to ask Miss Seton what it's all about, we go out on to the balcony and neither she nor I has the slightest idea that Zoller's out there on his side, with both hands cradling his ears. And when he gets the story, he uses his head – which I wish, oh how I wish Miss Seton had done – and he remembers that Rosamond Blake's ship puts in at Algeciras on its way to Lisbon. And he makes up his mind that he won't wait for Lord Lorrimer to get to Lisbon and interfere with the future plans of the star he's risking so much money on. He doesn't mind who she runs away with, just so long as she appears in the film – and he doesn't want any damaging publicity at this stage, and so he'll meet the boat at Algeciras and see what he can do. And he might do a lot; a woman who's midway between two big moments of her life, who's had time to think, who's been removed for a time from the handsome presence, might need very little to sway her one way or the other.'

'I only thought of stopping Lord Lorrimer,' said Miss Seton. 'I didn't want to interfere with Rosamond's life.'

'And that,' said Mr Holt, 'is a feminine statement, or I never heard one before.' He turned to Angus. 'My advice to you is: get rid of Tarrant, and fast. He won't care whether you know the facts or whether you don't – but just so long as he's on the coach, he's going to go on thinking up schemes and trying to make them work. These non-adult types can be as dangerous as real crooks, and all without meaning to. Get rid of him. You've got plenty of proof if you need it.'

'But if he gets rid of him,' objected Miss Seton, 'he'll go

straight to Angela and tell her everything.'

'I don't think he will,' said Mr Holt. 'He's not concerned with anything but the opportunity to have fun.'

When Angus left them, he stood for some moments in the corridor and let the full import of what he had heard fill his mind. His thoughts were confused, but one fact stood out clearly: trouble was coming to Angela.

Angela. She knew nothing, suspected nothing. And soon, her father would have to tell her. It was easy to see why he had not been able to tell her before the journey began. There had been nothing to tell. The idyll was over; he and Rosamond had parted – finally, he thought. And her letter must have reached him almost at the moment of his setting out to board the *Green Empress*. There would have been no time for any change of plan. It was no wonder that he had been travelling in agony of mind . . .

Angus brought himself back to the task immediately before him. He had something to do before he could shut himself away to think over all he had heard.

Turning, he went to Maurice Tarrant's room. Maurice, bidding him enter, greeted him with an amiable smile and waved a hand towards the bed. Angus saw on it all the things that had been in Maurice's locker on the coach.

'I had those taken out and brought upstairs,' said Maurice. 'I had a feeling the *Green Empress* would be going on without me.'

'That saves everybody a lot of trouble,' said Angus.

'I saw you and Holt going hotfoot in the direction of Miss Seton's room. Why? I asked myself.'

'You found the right answer. How do you propose to get to Lisbon?'

'Well, I've just gathered from the manager that I can keep on this room if you agree to let me have it. I understand that Hornblower and his sister are getting to Lisbon at the Company's expense, and I asked him if he'd take me along.'

'And he agreed?'

'Not exactly. But he said that it was obvious I couldn't be permitted to go on with the present set of passengers, having made myself so obnoxious – his word, and a nice one: obnoxious. He said I could go in their car and sit in front with the driver; if I so much as turned my head, he said, he'd knock it off. Nice prospect, I must say. One would think I'd committed a series of crimes.'

'You wanted to send Lord Lorrimer into the river.'

'My dear fellow, I didn't plan to hurt him!'

'Then what was the idea?'

'Well, when my delaying tactics fell flat, I reasoned that the chief thing that had attracted a world-famous beauty like Rosamond Blake was his handsome countenance and youthful appearance – so if she saw him with an old look, she might take a new look. In other words, if he arrived in Lisbon looking a bit the worse for wear, she'd think again. These old boys put on years after any kind of shock – look at the Admiral; falls down backwards and gets up looking ten years older. If Holt hadn't interfered, Lord Lorrimer would have taken a gentle roll into the river and been hauled out again and he would have arrived in Lisbon looking a bit more like the grandfather he's shortly going to be. The girl would have been instantly cured.'

'Neither you, not I, nor anybody else has the slightest right to interfere in this affair.'

'Why not? It isn't an affair between two ordinary people. The girl's at the top of the tree and the man's been there for years and they've both got a hell of a lot to lose. I don't care what he loses, but Rosamond Blake happens to be my favourite actress, and I think she's much too young and lovely to throw herself away on a dry old pod like Lorrimer. If he wants to have another kick at life, and if he's tired of his wife – who I daresay is very dull – let him choose some nice model who's trying to hit the headlines. I don't want him to be a good boy and go home; not at all. He can do what he likes, just so long as he keeps his aged paws off Rosamond. Is that sense, or is it what Holt calls non-sense?'

'It's sense – but niether you nor I have any right to try to make him see it. His life's his own. The fact that he's on his way to mess it up doesn't give his fellow-passengers the right to offer unwanted advice or to try to shape his destiny.'

'Well, you may be right, but I don't agree with you. You're not, by the way, going to put me on the *Empress* black list, are you? If I don't like the look of this Lisbon job – and something tells me I'm not going to – I've got to get home again, you know.'

'I shall report the fact that you arranged to leave the coach and travel with the Admiral. I'm a courier, not a probation officer.'

'If you're worrying about whether I'm going to tell Angela,

you needn't. You can set your mind – or do I mean your heart? – at rest. I won't breathe a word to her.'

'Goodbye,' said Angus.

'Oh, that's a harsh word. Let's keep it open,' suggested Maurice. 'Au revoir, my dear fellow. I was going to offer my congratulations, but let's keep that open, too.' He gave a wide, malicious grin. 'My dear Angus, I wouldn't be in your shoes for anything. Not for anything.'

Angus went out and closed the door – but he was not yet to find leisure for thought. Coming towards him was Mr Holt.

'Can I have a word with you?' he asked Angus.

'Of course. What is it?'

'Just this. I've . . . I've persuaded Miss Seton to leave the coach.'

Angus stared at him.

'To – ?'

'To leave the coach. It's what she ought to have done as soon as she got the news of her sister the other night. She ought to have told you what the news was, and asked you to arrange her journey back to England – or on to Lisbon by some other means. She oughtn't to have stayed, day after day, just watching Lord Lorrimer getting nearer to where he was going. I talked to her just now – and she's leaving the coach. And so,' concluded Mr Holt quietly, 'am I.'

'Both of you?'

'But naturally. Have you eyes, brother? If so, you must have seen that I don't dislike the girl. You fell in love on the trip, and so did I – or perhaps at my age, people don't fall; just say I drifted gently. I took a look, I liked what I saw.'

'And – and Miss Seton?' Angus could not help asking.

'Likes me. For the moment, that's all right with me. She's a cool hand, and that's one of the things I like about her. Maybe in other circumstances, I wouldn't have got so far so fast – but she needed someone to get her out of the mess she got into when she talked to Tarrant, and I'm glad I was there.' He took off his glasses, polished them and put them on again. 'Son,' he ended, 'you'll never know what I owe this *Green Empress*.'

'I'm sorry you're going.'

'Me, I'm glad. I've got a few things to say that I don't want the other passengers to overhear. But I'm sorry that this leaves the coach with more empty seats, and so Miss Seton and I plan to write a letter to the Company telling them that this series of accidents was nothing at all to do with you and that as a courier, you were fine.'

'Thank you. But – ',

'But what?'

'Nothing.'

It was no use trying to explain that Sir Claud would be quite unmoved by letters of explanation. Passengers did not drop off *Green Empress* coaches like fruit from a windswept tree. Passengers set out ten in number and arrived ten in number; the Company practically guaranteed it.

'Can I,' he asked Mr Holt, 'make any arrangements for you?'

'No, thanks – except to let the staff know that we're going on on our own. I can do the rest. My Spanish isn't spectacular, but it goes. I just want to thank you for all you've done – and I promised Miss Seton that I'd take you along to say goodbye to her. Will you come?'

'Of course. What,' he asked, as they went, 'does seven from ten leave?'

'Only three. But among them, remember, you've got your most important passenger, Lord Lorrimer. Just so long as you get him there safely, the Company won't lose any sleep over the rest of us.'

Angus let it pass.

CHAPTER 13

THEY were leaving Spain. Every mile was bringing them nearer to the borders of Portugal – and in the coach, Angus and the three remaining passengers sat silent, lost in their thoughts.

There was no scenery that could distract them. The stretch of road along which they were speeding was as straight as an airstrip, and almost as flat; on either side could occasionally be seen oak forest or pig farms, but the greater part of the landscape was bare and open: pastures, ranches on which fighting bulls were bred. There was little to see, and if there had been, nobody would have looked.

Angus was giving thanks for certain blessings: Ferdy, though depressed by the scant number of passengers left on the coach, placed the responsibility on Maurice Tarrant and – now that Maurice Tarrant was left behind – showed no suspicion that other factors might have been at work. Angela had questions to ask, but said nothing; seeing Angus's depression, she put it down to the loss of his passengers, and did not probe. And Lionel Yule was showing the detachment he had shown throughout the journey.

For the first time, Angus realised that trouble was in store for Yule; when he reached Lisbon, he was going to find himself without a job. He had lost Angela, and at the journey's end he was going to lose her father. There was no end to the unhappy chain: Angela, Yule, Miss Seton, the Zollers, the Admiral and his sister, Maurice Tarrant . . . and himself, mused Angus. They were all caught fast in the tangle.

His eyes rested on Lord Lorrimer's haggard face. If Rosamond Blake could see him now, she would hardly feel herself sufficient compensation for all that he was leaving behind. Struggling to condemn, as Miss Seton and Maurice Tarrant had condemned, Angus found himself with nothing but pity in his heart. It was a tragedy that a man of Lord Lorrimer's character and reputation had found himself, at fifty-five, in love with a young girl. This journey, he realised, must have been in the nature of a preliminary penance; a battleground between the past and the unknown future. Was it Rosamond he wanted, Angus wondered, or was it her youth . . . or his own? Having had so many good things in life, did he think that he could order the mixture as before? Did he imagine that his good looks and charm would be proof against Time's wear and tear? Fifty-five was an age at which a man might have twenty useful years before him – but a new life with a young girl?

Angus went back to the story Miss Seton had told. Her sister had rejected the proposal to go to South America with Lord Lorrimer – and then she had changed her mind. Her letter must have reached him the day before he was due to leave for Lisbon. No wonder he had sat throughout the journey looking as he had done.

Angus, for the hundredth time, examined his plan of breaking the news to Angela himself – and for the hundredth time, rejected it. The secret was not his; it was her father's, and only her father had the right to break it to her in his own way – but not, decided Angus, in his own time. He had been shut away too long, brooding. He must come out of his musings and learn that the affair no longer involved himself alone. He must tell Angela the truth – and when he had told it, Angus would comfort her.

He looked out to see the coach slowing up at the approach to Ciudad Rodrigo. They got out and waited for lunch, but when it came it was a quiet meal; nobody seemed disposed to talk. Before the coach left for the frontier, Angus had a few moments alone with Angela.

'You're still looking terribly depressed,' she told him anxiously.

'That's because I am depressed.'

'I know. It's nice, isn't it, to think that in future we'll never have to face trouble alone?'

He looked down at her.

'Just so long as you remember that . . . ' he said slowly.

'These have been beastly days for you. I wish I could have done something.'

'You were here – that was enough. But when trouble comes to you, remember that I'm there to share it.'

'You mean I just hand it to you and let you deal with it?'

'Yes.'

'We share all the joys and you bear all the troubles?'

'Yes again. Will you remember that?'

'Of course I will.'

She sat with him in the little observation compartment until they reached the frontier. The formalities on the Spanish side ended, they drove slowly to where the Portuguese officials awaited them; they looked darker, sterner than the Spaniards, but the country was infititely softer and greener.

Past the frontier, the road became steeper; the air, which had been almost oppressive during the afternoon, became pleasantly cool. The coach climbed, and then they could see, across a narrow valley, the *Green Empress* hotel, set amid trees, in which they were to spend the night.

Ferdy, handing over the few remaining pieces of luggage, had a gloomy comment to make.

'We started out with thirty-four cases, sir.'

'Yes, Ferdy; I know.'

'Now we're down to eleven. What's the Company going to think, sir?' He sighed. 'I know it's none of your fault, sir, but in all the years I've been with them, I've never known any-thing like this happen. Never. We've gone off with ten passengers and we've arrived with ten, all intact. We've had a troublesome passenger or two, asking for this and that, but asking to leave the coach? Never, sir; never.'

'Nobody's made any complaints against the coach, Ferdy.'

'I know, sir, but back at Head Office, where they keep the numbers, that's all they'll look at, sir. We've lost seven passengers, sir, and that's . . . that's phee-nominal.'

'I daresay it is, but there's nothing we can do about it. Mr and Mrs Zoller left to make a quick trip to Algeciras; the Admiral was injured and his sister wasn't well. Mr Tarrant went because he tried to be too funny. Mr Holt and Miss Seton – well, I leave you to guess. On paper it might look bad, but you're in the clear, Ferdy. The only thing that could affect the Company's credit is complaints – and there aren't any. Everybody has been most careful to say so.'

'To you, sir, and to me; what's important is that they should say so to Sir Claud.'

Angus smiled down at the sturdy figure.

'I've let you down, Ferdy, and I'm sorry.'

'You haven't done anything wrong, sir.'

'Neither did Jonah, but the fact that he was there seemed to cause a lot of trouble. They heaved him overboard, so perhaps it's as well I'm only doing the job for one trip – or two, if they let me do the return journey.'

'I think you've made a good job of it, sir, barring these accidents.'

'Well, we've got the most important passenger with us still. If we get Lord Lorrimer there safely, we'll get a few marks. Send the luggage in, Ferdy, and don't worry about anything. I'll ask Lord Lorrimer to send a special message to Sir Claud giving us both a good write-up.'

He walked into the hotel, frowning as he went. The exchange, short though it had been, crystallised his decision to speak to Lord Lorrimer. The thing had gone on long enough; they were all involved, and Ferdy was the last to be caught; he was out there now wondering whether his job was safe.

He would go at once, he decided, to Lord Lorrimer's room; ne would tell him the whole story and ask his permission to break the news to Angela.

Only one duty remained before he was free: the distribution of mail. There was nothing for anybody but Lionel Yule; Angus sent a servant to his room with the telegram and then went upstairs to Lord Lorrimer's room.

Knocking, he was told to enter. When he went in, he found Lord Lorrimer looking at him in surprise.

'That was quick,' he commented.

'Quick, sir?'

'I've just this moment sent a message asking you to come and see me. Didn't you get it?'

'No, sir. I . . . I came because I had something rather important to say to you.'

A short silence fell. Lord Lorrimer looked at the younger man and took in slowly his pallor, his hesitation and his air of strain.

'Perhaps,' he said, 'what I have to say to you won't be such a shock, after all.'

Angus's expression did not change.

'What did you want to say to me, sir?'

Before answering, Lord Lorrimer turned and walked slowly to the window and stood staring across the valley. When he faced Angus and spoke, his first question was not a direct one.

'When Miss Seton left the coach this morning, did she give any reason?'

'Yes, sir. She did.'

Lord Lorrimer smiled – a grim, bitter smile, and Angus felt his heart beating faster with relief. He was going to speak. He was going to break his long silence; the matter was going to be brought to the surface. Angus resolved that before he left the other man, he would have extracted from him permission to tell Angela the truth in his own way.

'Once or twice,' said Lord Lorrimer, half to himself, 'I wondered about her. The name – Seton. But it seemed too great a coincidence. I didn't think it was possible. But – I was wrong, I suppose? She is Rosamond Blake's sister?'

'Yes, sir.'

'And . . . she told you?'

'She – '

Angus paused. There was much to tell, and Miss Seton's revelation was not the beginning of the story. And as he hesitated, wondering how he should begin, he heard a swift rush of footsteps and saw the door burst open – and knew that it was too late.

Angela stood before them, and as he looked at her, Angus realised that Maurice Tarrant had indeed kept his word. He had not told her – but he had done something far more effective: he had told Yule. Unwilling to leave the game at its most interesting stage, he had merely passed the ball to Yule, and Yule . . .

And in that moment, Angus found the answer to something that had puzzled him throughout the journey. Miss Seton had said that she did not trust Yule – and now he knew why. She had recognised, beneath the reliable-looking exterior, the man's essential weakness. Steady enough in ordinary circumstances, in an emergency Yule would fail – as he had failed now. He had received Tarrant's telegram, and his first thought had been for himself and for his position. He had told Angela the truth, confident that only she could at this stage prevent her father from carrying out his plans.

Yule had told her – as Tarrant had known that he would. And she was facing them now, white-faced, with something like horror in her eyes.

For a moment, she stood unmoving – then she had taken a few steps and her arms were round her father's neck.

'Lionel said – ' Her voice was stifled. 'Lionel said . . . he said . . . ' She raised her head and looked at him. 'It isn't true? It can't be true!'

Lord Lorrimer's face was ashen. He put up his arms and gently disengaged hers.

'Angela, will you let me explain?'

'Explain? Darling, you don't have to explain. I only want want to know whether it's true! You can tell me in one word whether this . . . Is it true that you left home to – to run away with . . . Oh, darling, is it true?'

'Quite true,' he said quietly. 'But – '

'And you knew!' She had swung round to face Angus. 'You knew! Lionel says that you knew. You knew that Maurice Tarrant and the others were doing everything they could to – to prevent it, to prevent my father from getting to Lisbon in time, and you . . . you said nothing, not one word, to me! That's true too, isn't it?'

'That's true,' said Angus, as quietly as her father had spoken. 'But if you'll – '

She took a step and came closer to him, speaking in a low, clear voice.

'I'd like to get this straight,' she said. 'It's . . . it's rather important. You knew that my father was breaking up his home, leaving his wife, leaving his children – one of whom was a lifelong friend of yours, and the other your fiancée – leaving them to run away with another woman. You – '

'Angela, will you let me explain?' broke in Lord Lorrimer.

'No,' she said quietly. 'This is between Angus and my-self.' She had not taken her eyes from Angus's face. 'You knew?' she asked him again.

'Yes, I knew.

'And all the time, you were with me, making love to me, talking to me about our future, holding me in your arms – and saying nothing whatsoever about the thing that was going on all round us, the thing that was to change my father's life, and my mother's life, and my brother's, and mine. You didn't say a single word. You behaved as though nothing was happening – nothing that could affect us – you and me – at all. You could do that – to me!'

'Angela – ' he began.

'What my father does in a matter of this kind,' she went on, unheeding, 'is principally between himself and my mother. But you – ' Her voice became strangled, and tears poured down her cheeks – 'you were different. You and I . . . You had said that you loved me, wanted to marry me – but if you had really loved me, you would have trusted me. You would have told me. But you said nothing. I might have been a child . . . or an idiot. Everybody knew . . . everybody – but I didn't know because you didn't trust me enough to tell me the truth.'

'Angela – ' Angus took a step forward. 'Angela, will you please listen?'

'No.' Her voice was quiet. 'No, I won't listen – not any more. What you do – what you both do . . . I don't care any more. I want to – to get away. I'm not going to sit watching us get nearer and nearer, as you've done. I'm not . . . '

She turned and went swiftly to the door. Her father's voice, sharp and angry, rang out.

'Angela – come back!'

She did not pause. She went to the door, opened it, and then turned to say a last quiet sentence to Angus.

'I – I hope you'll be very happy, wherever you are. In England, or in . . . in Canada. But I don't . . . I don't want to see you again.'

The door closed. Angus took a step towards it, and Lord Lorrimer spoke.

'One moment.'

Angus turned.

'I don't understand,' said Lord Lorrimer. 'She said . . . she said that everybody knew. What did she mean?'

Angus told him.

Standing there, he related exactly what had occurred since Miss Seton received the call from her mother. He told of her distress and her first foolish reaction, which was to delay the coach. He spoke of her ill-advised attempt, and Maurice Tarrant's subsequent actions. He described the attempts to enter the garage, the loss of the despatch case and the luggage, and their recovery. He spoke of Mr Holt and his interest in Miss Seton and discovery of Tarrant's activities. He spoke as briefly as he could; he gave nothing but the bare facts, touching on the departure of the Zollers and the suspicions of the Admiral. He ended by relating his conversation with Mr Holt, and the latter's decision to persuade Miss Seton to leave the coach.

When he had finished, he found himself wandering to the window and staring out, as Lord Lorrimer had stared. After one glance, he felt unable to face the other man's white, stricken face, with its look of sick realisation; he did not want to meet his defeated eyes. Lord Lorrimer was no longer looking at the past or at the future; he was staring, with shocked anguish, at the present.

Angus did not know how long he stood at the window. When at last the other man spoke, he turned.

'I'm sorry,' Lord Lorrimer was saying, in a quiet voice. 'I'm sorry to have been the cause of so much trouble to you . . . and to everybody.' He passed a hand wearily across his face. 'I suppose you've been through hell, wondering how Angela would feel when I . . . when I told her.'

'I knew that you must tell her soon. I came in here this evening to ask your permission to tell her myself.'

'When did Tarrant tell Yule?'

'There was a telegram for him; I sent it in just before I came in here to see you. It was from Tarrant, I suppose.'

'How did . . . how did Miss Seton come to be on the coach?'

'It was a last-minute decision. She was going to surprise her sister.'

'And day after day,' said Lord Lorrimer, 'I sat there without a thought of what was going on all round me. Day after day, I sat there thinking that this was a matter between three people: my wife and myself – and . . .'

'Perhaps I ought to be sorry that you brought Angela with

you – but if you hadn't brought her, I wouldn't have met her again.'

'What else could I do, in God's name, but bring her? I got the letter exactly eighteen hours before the time we were due to leave. When I left Italy, it was with no thought that we would ever meet again. All I wanted to do was forget. I'd tried in a hundred different ways to tell my wife – and I couldn't. So I had decided to put it all behind me. When the letter came . . . '

He stopped. When he spoke again, his voice was quiet.

'Go and bring Angela back,' he said. 'She can't be allowed to go away without speaking to me – or to you. Go and bring her to me.'

Angus went in search of her. She was not in her room. She was not, he found at last, in the hotel. Ferdy, his eyes warm with sympathy, broke the news: she had driven away with Yule. They had taken their luggage and they had gone in the direction of Guarda.

He went back to Lord Lorrimer and told him, in one quiet sentence, what had happened. They looked at one another, measuring the extent of the damage. Then the older man gave a brief, mirthless laugh.

'Odd, isn't it? You walk into something without warning. It hits you, and you go down. You look to the world like an old man snatching greedily at youth and romance, and instead, what are you? A man fighting a losing battle, trying to hold on to everything he's built up, and seeing it go to pieces – and seeing the ruin spreading . . . and spreading. To her sister, to those others, to Angela – and now to you.'

He stopped. Leaning his hands upon the table, he stared unseeingly at the brightly-polished surface. Then he straightened and looked at Angus.

'Can't we get out of here? Can't we . . . get on? Can't we go, move, leave this place?'

'Now, sir?'

'Why not? We're due in Lisbon tomorrow evening. If we go now, and drive all night, we'll get there in the morning. The date would be the same, and I don't suppose the Company would quibble if the coach arrived a few hours earlier than scheduled. Do you want to spend the night here?'

'No.'

'Neither do I. For God's sake, let's go on and get to the end of this accursed journey. I'm ready to go now, if you are.'

'I'll make the arrangements,' said Angus.

He went to consult Ferdy, and found him not only willing, but anxious to go on.

'We'll arrive a bit ahead of schedule, sir, but that won't worry the Company. It's being late they'd object to.'

'You don't mind the night drive?'

'I'll enjoy it, sir. This has been an unlucky trip, and I'll feel happier when it's over.'

The hotel staff were only too eager to see them set off: a runaway couple, a pursuit; it was in the best romantic tradition. Ferdy, his own apprehensions for the future drowned in a rush of sympathy for Angus, tried to assemble some words of sympathy, failed, shook his head mournfully and set about his preparations for departure.

Angus, going mechanically through the usual formalities, fought again and again with the waves of panic that swept into his mind. He had failed her, and she had gone away. He had looked at the situation from one point of view and he had acted for what he felt was the best. But she . . . she saw his silence as betrayal and she had gone away.

He finished his preparations and went downstairs. Ferdy departed to bring round the *Empress*, and a message was sent to Lord Lorrimer that all was ready.

Angus walked out of the hotel and stood on the drive, his eyes following the road that wound among the hills, searching for a sign of the car in which was the girl who only last night had rested in his arms, whose lips had warmed beneath his own. He moved restlessly across the drive and mounted a grassy slope to get a better view of the valley. Below him, the drive made a steep upward curve, dropping as steeply to the hotel entrance. He saw a break in the trees opposite, and stepped on to the drive to get a better view.

She was there . . . somewhere. She had gone, and he and her father, without wasting time on discussion, had known that it was no use going after her. She was hurt, and she was angry. She had gone – where? She could go back to Spain, or she could go on to Lisbon. She would recover, soon, from the first effects of the news, and then she would begin to think, and begin to judge. She would not judge her father – but she would judge the man to whom she had given her generous, impulsive heart. She had given liberally – and she felt that he had given nothing in return.

Searching miserably among the ruins of the past few days,

he wondered whether there was any moment at which he could have staved off disaster. He could have made a better estimate of Tarrant's capacity for mischief. He could have shown more active sympathy with Miss Seton, and drawn from her the story which she had so unwisely told Tarrant. But having learnt the cause of her distress, would he have told Angela?

He thought not. He was still certain that he had had no right to speak before her father spoke. He would not have told her. If the past few days could be re-enacted, he would do again what he had done before. And in the end, she would have gone . . . gone away.

For a few moments, apprehension, misery, fear rushed together in his mind and made him insensible to his surroundings. A brief, bitter vision of the future rose before him, a future without Angela. He closed his eyes and fought to conquer the panic that threatened to overwhelm him – and at that moment, Ferdy brought the *Green Empress* down the steep curve of the drive.

Events, for the next twenty seconds, moved swiftly, drastically and inevitably. Angus heard a shout, and turned to find the coach almost on him. He had only to leap – and he leapt. But in springing aside, he acted instinctively and with no remembrance of the precautions which since his accident had been necessary. He sprang – and then he knew that his injured knee was not going to take his weight.

He heard other shouts, and had a second's glimpse of Ferdy's wide, staring eyes. The coach swerved, lurched – and then there was a sound of crashing branches, followed by a long, peaceful silence.

Lying in the ditch, Angus felt that his mind was working with remarkable clarity. It was comfortable down there, he mused. Interesting, too: it was obvious that Ferdy kept the underside of the *Empress* as impeccable as he kept the bodywork. Good old Ferdy. No sign of him; perhaps he was looking for him and hadn't thought of looking in the ditch. One should yell . . . in a moment or two.

Ditch . . . There was something, after all, in this psychic business. The Admiral's sister had seen it all. She'd seen a Spanish ditch, of course, and this was a Portuguese ditch – and it wasn't the Admiral who was under the coach; it was himself. Apart from those little details, it was an amazingly accurate forecast.

One should try to get out – but perhaps not. Wouldn't do to disturb the *Green Empress*; she was hanging over him and she looked a bit precariously balanced. Wonder what she'd weigh? Must work it out some time. Some other time . . .

From a great distance, he heard voices, and presently he identified Lord Lorrimer's.

'Angus! Angus – can you hear me?'

'I . . . Yes.'

'Thank God. Are you . . . are you all right?'

'Alive and well,' said Angus.

'Thank God,' said Lord Lorrimer again.

If that was a prayer, count him in, thought Angus. If the ditch had been a foot wider, if the two front wheels had gone down instead of going over . . .

Strong hands were pushing supports beneath the coach. Gentle hands were pulling him out, inch by inch. The underside of the *Empress* gave way to the branches of trees, and then to the pale, beautiful, welcome sky, and then the sky was obscured by Lord Lorrimer's drawn, haggard face.

'Angus – are you all right?'

'Perfectly. Ferdy?'

'He was thrown out. He's unconscious, but I don't think he's injured. Lie still while the doctor looks you over.'

Angus struggled to a sitting position.

'I'm all right. It was my knee, my blasted knee. Weak-kneed . . . '

With the help of those round him, he got to his feet. Not far away, Ferdy was lying, the picture of repose. On his back among the undergrowth, eyes closed, hands clasped on his stomach, he looked like a man sleeping off the effects of a picnic lunch.

'We'll get him inside,' said Lord Lorrimer.

Angus limped across and bent over the driver. Ferdy's eyes opened and he lay gazing up at Angus, his look, at first blank, gradually showing signs of returning consciousness.

'Sir?'

'How are you, Ferdy?'

'I'm fine, sir,' said Ferdy, and proved it by lapsing back into unconsciousness.

They bore him gently indoors and laid him on a bed. His eyes opened once more, and went from one to the other of the anxious faces round him, resting at last on Angus.

'You all right, sir?'

'Yes. It was my fault, Ferdy, and I'm sorry.'

'*Empress* all right, sir?'

'She's fine.' It was Lord Lorrimer who answered. 'She jumped the ditch and she's got a scratch or two, but nothing more.'

Ferdy nodded, and spoke in a firm voice to Angus.

'You've got to go on, sir.'

'We'll all go on, Ferdy, when you're feeling a bit less shaken.'

'I'm all right, sir. But I can't drive today or tomorrow. Muzzy, like. Will you take the *Empress* to Lisbon, sir?'

'There's no need for that, Ferdy. I'll drive it if you like, but you can come too.'

'No, sir. I'll follow you. You've got to get his lordship to Lisbon. Rules of the Company, sir; if the driver hits any trouble, the courier takes over. You take over, sir, and get his lordship to Lisbon.'

Angus glanced at Lord Lorrimer.

'Your knee?' the latter asked.

'I could drive.' He looked at Ferdy. 'But –'

'There's no But, sir,' came firmly from Ferdy. 'I'll follow you in a few days.'

'We've got a day in hand, Ferdy,' Angus reminded him.

'Yes, sir, but you'll need that to take her slowly; you're not used to handling her, like I am.' His eyes besought Angus. 'Everything's happened this trip, sir, but the *Empress* can still arrive on time. That's all we can do now, sir – get her in on time. Don't wait till tomorrow, sir; start now, and take her slowly and give yourself a rest on the way. Will you do it, sir?'

Angus met the earnest, appealing gaze.

'All right, Ferdy, I'll do it.'

When they had seen to his comfort, they drove away. Angus was at the wheel. Lord Lorrimer sat alone in the coach. They could not communicate and perhaps, thought Angus, it was as well that they could not; they had, at this moment, nothing to say to one another. Angus set his mind to studying the route and the performance of the coach, striving to ignore the stabs that memory, every now and then, dealt out to him.

It was over, and he wasn't, in a way, surprised, he told himself. It had been, from the beginning, an improbable sort of dream: he had been a courier, and a beautiful girl had thrown her arms about his neck and said to him: 'I've loved you ever since I first met you; I'm yours.' They had embraced, and she had said: 'Let's rent a castle in Spain,' and he had agreed, knowing all the time that he was asleep and that sooner or later he must wake – to reality. And he had wakened, and she had gone, as he had known she would be gone, and all that remained now was to keep one's eye on the future and one's mind off the past. She was gone. Angela . . . Angela was gone.

He fought to keep her out of his mind. But he could not prevent the ghosts in the coach from holding a ghoulish autopsy.

'Under the coach,' shrieked the Admiral's sister. 'Under the coach, under the coach, under the coach.'

'The pig,' said Mr Zoller, 'must be pregnant.'

'I don't trust him,' moaned Miss Seton. 'I don't trust him.'

'There's a time for talking,' said Mr Holt, 'and a time for not talking.'

'I wouldn't be in your shoes for anything,' yelled Maurice Tarrant. 'I wouldn't, I wouldn't . . .'

'Got him!' shouted the Admiral. 'Got him, got him!'

Angus tore his mind away. Lovely names, these Portuguese ones: *Celorico da Beira*; perhaps it meant something. Fork in the road: did they want N.16 or N.17? N.17, obviously; they were heading for Coimbra. They had been scheduled to stop there for lunch tomorrow, the whole round dozen of them: ten passengers, one courier, one driver. Ten passengers . . . the Zollers, the Admiral and his sister, Miss Seton and Mr Holt and Lord Lorrimer and Yule and Tarrant . . . and Angela. Angela. Better get used to saying it. There were a lot of girls called Angela, and one might have to use the name, and if one couldn't bring it out, it would look odd. Angela. Angela, Angela, Angela. Oh God, Angela . . .

Pleasant country, Portugal. Especially at dawn. They didn't waste any space; crops and more crops, and if it wasn't vines, it was cork, and if it wasn't cork, it was olives. Roadmen every few yards, wide-brimmed hats, happy smile, polite salute.

A tap on the window from Lord Lorrimer; a stop. A cigarette, and then on again, with scarcely a word spoken. Coimbra ahead: University – and something else. Yes, the Villa of Tears, *Quinta das Lagrimas*, where they'd murdered

Inez da Castro in 1355. That was a long time ago; nobody, now, shed tears in the villa. Time healed. Inez . . . Angela.

And now no more journeying to the west; turn south, down, down to Lisbon. '*Well, I shall face that way, and then I shall know that south is behind me and east is on my right hand.*'

Stop to buy food. Half each; back to the coach, eat as you go.

Leiria . . . what was that? The Roman Calippo. Captured by the Moors in 1135. Odd how a man could have a brain for history and be totally deficient in other knowledge: how to keep love safe, for example. How to keep his love close to him, attached by – what was it? – hoops of steel, so that whatever came, she would stay by him. Whatever happened, whatever he did, just so long as he did it thinking it was the right thing to do.

Nazaré off to the right. Fishermen with checked shirts and traditions lost in Phoenician times. Oxen pulling boats up the beach, boats with eyes painted on the prow.

Alijubarrota somewhere about here. Great day for the Irish? No, the Portuguese. King John gains independence of country from Castile, August 14th, 1385. Didn't do to have too good a memory. One had to forget, sometimes – push things away, put them up in a trunk in the attic and take them out again years and years later, when you could begin to bear it, when it had become a lavender-scented memory, and not this searing kind.

Alcobaca. Batalha. One thing about driving, it kept a part of your mind busy. How many hours? The sun wasn't as high as it had been. This time yesterday, he and Angela . . .

The last few miles. Lisbon ahead, and the *Empress* in good shape internally, but showing a few scars on her hitherto unblemished sides. A dent, a scratch or two, not too noticeable in any other vehicle, perhaps, but the last step in humiliation for a *Green Empress*.

But he had brought her in. He was a few hours early, but Lord Lorrimer would have to argue about that – if he could find time. For himself, he didn't care much any more. He had done his best to uphold Sir Claud's standards, and they were still flying; they were tattered and even a little bloody, but here was the *Green Empress* on her way up the Avenida da Liberdade, with her most important passenger still aboard, and the others lost somewhere along the route. Lost . . . lost. Oh God, Angela.

Perhaps he was tired. There wasn't much more to do. Drive Lord Lorrimer to the *Green Empress* hotel and leave him there. Hand over his luggage. Two suitcases – out of thirty-something. Try to say something, and then decide there wasn't anything much to say except something about Good Luck. He'd need it. They'd both need it.

And then there was the last duty; properly Ferdy's, but now his: to drive the *Empress* to her garage and hand her over.

Not as easy as it sounded, driving her into that vast place with three other *Green Empresses* looking on disdainfully. Who was this bedraggled sister? Well, a lick of paint and she'd be almost herself again.

The *Green Empress* was home. And for himself – what was the address? No, thank you, he didn't want a lift; he'd find his own way. Did he report here about the return journey, or to the office? To the office? Right. He'd do that in a day or two . . . or three or four, when he'd had a bath, or eaten, or slept, or all three. Goodbye. Sorry about the damage, explain later. Goodbye.

He reached his quarters and was taken up to his room. His suitcase was brought up, but he scarcely saw it; he was looking at the wide, inviting bed.

He sat down, kicked off his shoes and lay back. He closed his eyes and let memory and misery flood over him. It was over. It was all over. She had been sweet, and generous, and he would love her as long as he lived, and remember her graciousness and her beauty. But she didn't want him any more. He had failed her. He would never work out exactly how, but he had failed her and it was finished.

He ordered food, and it was brought, but when it was set down on the table in his room, he did not see it. Sleep had closed in on him; sleep, merciful and all-obscuring. Unhappiness, weariness, hopelessness were all submerged in the gentle waves of sleep. He sank slowly, deeply, deeply . . .

CHAPTER 14

WHEN he opened his eyes, it was to see Wax Sealing in a chair beside the bed.

He lay still, eyes half open, watching Wax watching him. Wax said nothing and did nothing to hasten his return to full consciousness; he merely got up, rang the bell and waited for a servant to answer it.

'Two breakfasts,' he ordered.

Angus sat up with a jerk.

'*Breakfasts?*'

'Breakfasts.'

'What the hell's the time?'

'Ten-thirty on the morning of Thursday the twenty-sixth of May,' chanted Wax. 'Good morning, children, everywhere.'

'Where did you come from?' demanded Angus.

'They flew me out.'

There was a pause.

'I see,' said Angus at last. 'As a courier, I'm through?'

'As a courier, you've made Company history. But though some of us are grateful to you, Sir Claud feels that you're not quite cut out for the job. You've got – I quote him – certain peculiarities which the Company does not care to exploit.'

'So I'm out?'

Wax looked shocked.

'We do not "out" anybody.'

'Well, am I still on the payroll or am I not?'

'You are. You'll get paid for the return journey, but – '

' – but I make my own way back, is that it?'

'If you'd let me finish a sentence, Angus old boy, instead of putting unkind thoughts into poor old Sir Claud's head, we'd get this settled in no time. You get paid for the return journey, and we take you back. All we ask, all we beg, in fact, is that you confine yourself to sitting in one of our Deepfoam seats and enjoying the scenery. We don't ask you to perform the functions of a courier.'

'That's what I said: I'm out.'

'You're being taken home on the next available seat on the next available *Empress*, and in the meantime Sir Claud asks me to tell you' – Wax grinned – 'that we have several quiet homes for tired couriers. You've got about two weeks to put in, and you needn't spend them in Lisbon unless you particularly want to.'

'I don't want to.'

'In that case, you can choose one of the outlying houses we place at the disposal of couriers who fall ill. There's a small house with a small staff up near Fatima. There's another near Setubal. For mental cases, there's a splendid one you'd like; it's – '

'All I want,' said Angus, 'is to get right away.'

'Ah. Right away from what?'

'From people. Give me the address of a place I can stay in that's right away from everything and everybody, and I'll stay there until it's time to go home. I don't want a staff.'

'There's a beach hut over on the other side of the river, but – '

'But what?'

'You could hole up there and spend your time going in and out of the sea, but you'd have to walk into the village and get your food and your mail.'

Angus walked into the bathroom and turned on the taps.

'That's the one,' he said.

'But what about people being able to get at you if they want to?'

'They won't want to.' Angus was stripping off his clothes. 'If anybody wants to see me . . . particularly . . . they can drop me a line and I'll take the next bus back to Lisbon.'

There was a pause. Angus soaped vigorously, and Wax poured out his coffee and carried it to the bathroom.

'I don't want to tear aside any veils,' he said, 'but rumour's rumour and there's an awful lot of it around. If you don't want to talk about it, of course I'll respect your wish, but I'll be terribly disappointed. Wasn't there a girl called Angela?'

Angus enveloped himself in a large bath sheet and looked directly at his friend.

'The whole thing,' he said, 'was a nice dream and all I want is a bit of time in which to . . . to wake up.'

Wax said nothing. They ate breakfast in silence, and then he spoke slowly.

'One thing you ought to know,' he said, 'is that Lord Lorrimer is going back to England.'

'And that,' said Angus, 'was sticking out a mile all the

way from Guarda to Lisbon. His first mistake was in falling in love with the Spring. His second – a bad one – was not to reply at once by telegram to the suggestion that reached him the day before he left London. It was a dead wicket and he knew it – but I suppose you can't tell that to a beautiful woman who's decided she wants you after all. His wife will forgive him – she's the forgiving kind; she's also the kind that won't be any the worse for a shaking up. They'll both be on an *Empress* soon – I'll bet on it, if you like – having a second honeymoon.'

'But this girl Angela – '

'She's laid a girlhood ghost. And now if you'll give me the address of this beach hut, I'll get myself out to it.'

'And – '

' – and if anybody wants me, send me word and I'll come.'

He spent two weeks in the hut, alone, almost at peace. The sea was cold, but the sand was warm; he bathed, lay on the beach and bathed again. He fetched food and wine from the cluster of tiny houses half a mile from the hut. He saw groups of small, dark, curious children; he heard the sound of cars on the road above, but nothing led to his beach but a steep, broken path, and he remained undisturbed. Each day he walked up the path and met the bus that brought the letters. Sometimes there was some mail for him, but there was never the letter he looked for. There was no word, no message. It was over.

He went back to Lisbon as he had come, carrying his suitcase up the path and climbing aboard the bus for the journey to the ferry at Cacilhas. Across the river was Lisbon, and soon he was walking back to the hotel to await instructions from Wax.

There were letters on his table; he picked them up and looked swiftly through the envelopes. Nothing. A small, stubborn hope, that had persisted in spite of all his efforts, died.

Wax was not long in appearing.

'Tomorrow, ten-thirty,' he said. 'How d'you feel?'

'I feel fine. How's Ferdy?'

'Ferdy's fine too. But one or two people wanted to see you. As they weren't the person I thought you'd particularly want to see, I told them that you were incommunicado.'

'If you used that word, you're the one who ought to go to the place they keep for mental breakdowns.'

'The Admiral and his sister are still here. And so is Tarrant
– but not for long.'

'He didn't like the job.'

'No.'

'Well, that doesn't surprise me. If he's going home on an
Empress, it had better be under strong escort.'

'It is. He's travelling with the Admiral. He calls him sir.
If you're interested, the Zollers are in Lisbon too, looking
very pleased with themselves. They were photographed arm
in arm with Rosamond Blake just before she went off to
South America.'

'Did you see anything of Miss Seton?'

'She was in the photograph too.'

'What became of Holt?'

'He was in the photograph too. They were all in the photograph.'

'I see. Well, before I go back, I'd like to thank you for
getting me the job. I'm sorry I made a hash of it.'

'It wasn't your hash; everybody knows that. Incidentally,
I'm your courier.'

'Good. I'll watch you and see just where I went wrong.'

He arrived at the departure point shortly before half past
ten on the following morning. Waiting outside the hotel stood
the *Green Empress*, its colour blending pleasantly with the
soft hues of the garden. Beside it, talking to Wax, was a
stout, familiar figure, and Angus, after staring for a moment
in astonishment, went forward with hand outstretched.

'Ferdy! Are you driving us?'

'I am, sir.' Ferdy's face beamed. 'I asked Mr Sealing if I
could take you back. Be like old times, sir.'

'I sincerely hope not,' said Wax. 'I've told Mr Graham
that he's to keep his seat and watch the scenery – and you'll
watch the road. That way, we'll stay out of trouble.'

Ferdy grinned.

'Come and look at the *Empress*, sir,' he invited Angus.
'Good as new.'

'I wasn't sure whether she was the same *Empress* or not.'

'And that, if you don't mind me saying so, sir, is the difference between us drivers and you gentlemen. You couldn't
get a driver in the Company that didn't know, after his first
trip, exactly which *Empress* he'd handled.'

'But don't they all look alike?'

'To you, sir, maybe. To us . . . no.' Ferdy patted the side of the coach affectionately. 'She's my bus, sir, and I'd know her anywhere.'

They peered at the places in which she had been wounded, and saw no least mark or sign. She was her old, sleek self. Ferdy started the engine and she purred contentedly.

'Hear that, sir?' He beamed at Angus. 'That's the sound I like to hear.'

Wax appeared round the side of the coach.

'Passengers aboard,' he announced. 'Are you two thinking of joining us?'

Angus followed him round to the door. Wax, with mock ceremony, waved him on.

'After you, sir.'

Angus paused for a last look round. He had stood, as Wax was standing, not so long ago, ready to board the *Empress*, ready to take charge, ready to assume the responsibilities of the trip. Now he was going back without responsibilities, with only memories.

The scene misted for a few seconds. The gentle hum of the coach faded as the ghosts crowded round him. He heard the Admiral and his sister; he heard Mr Holt's unhurried sentences. Miss Seton, with her poise; Mrs Zoller, with her jewels. Maurice Tarrant's uninhibited speech. And Angela . . .

Pain gripped him. Wax, watching him, saw his face whiten, and put a gentle hand on his arm.

'All aboard,' he said, softly.

Angus stepped on to the coach.

For a moment, looking to left and right through a fog of confusion, he thought that the ghosts had come aboard with him. He put out a hand and gripped the back of a seat, and a horny hand reached out and covered his own.

'Well, well, well,' boomed the Admiral.

Angus tore himself out of his mists. As his vision cleared, he saw the one empty seat and began to walk slowly towards it.

He had walked thus many times. He had passed up this aisle and he knew exactly who would be seated to right and to left. His throat too tight to allow him to reply to the words of greeting from his old passengers, he went to the only empty seat, which had been Angela's.

He sat down. Here she had sat, and in front of her there had been Lionel Yule, and in front of Yule, Lord Lorrimer. And Lord Lorrimer was there now, opposite the smiling Miss Seton – but in the seat behind him there was not Yule. Yule was missing, and in his place was a slim figure, and Angus could see the back of a head that he had once thought too fair. Round it was a narrow band, a band that was not a ribbon, but a scarf. A scarf gay with little fans . . .

There was silence throughout the coach – the silence of happy expectancy. For Angus had put his hand on the chair in front of him, and was slowly turning it, turning it until he saw the fair face, the eyes, so unexpectedly brown, and glistening now with tears.

'If there's anything you want, sir . . . ' came Wax's voice from an immense distance.

A SELECTION OF FINE READING
AVAILABLE IN CORGI BOOKS

Novels

War

☐ 552 09223 1	365 DAYS	*Ronald J. Glasser M.D.* 40p
☐ 552 08874 9	SS GENERAL	*Sven Hassel* 35p
☐ 552 09178 2	REIGN OF HELL	*Sven Hassel* 35p
☐ 552 09245 2	BEWARE THE WOUNDED TIGER	*Geoff Taylor* 30p
☐ 552 08986 9	DUEL OF EAGLES (illustrated)	*Peter Townsend* 50p
☐ 552 09260 6	FINALE AT FLENSBURG (illustrated)	*Charles Whiting* 35p
☐ 552 09222 3	BEYOND THE TUMULT (illustrated)	*Barry Winchester* 40p

Romance

☐ 552 09207 X	THE GREEN EMPRESS	*Elizabeth Cadell* 30p
☐ 552 09208 8	BRIDAL ARRAY	*Elizabeth Cadell* 30p
☐ 552 09209 6	SPRING GREEN	*Elizabeth Cadell* 30p
☐ 552 09228 2	THE SEVEN SLEEPERS	*Kate Norway* 30p
☐ 552 09248 7	THE FARTHER OFF FROM ENGLAND	*Jean Ure* 30p

Science Fiction

☐ 552 09237 1	FANTASTIC VOYAGE	*Isaac Asimov* 35p
☐ 552 09238 X	FAHRENHEIT 451	*Ray Bradbury* 35p
☐ 552 09236 3	DRAGONFLIGHT	*Anne McCaffrey* 35p
☐ 552 09239 8	MORE THAN HUMAN	*Theodore Sturgeon* 35p

General

☐ 552 09251 7	OLDER TEENAGERS' SEX QUESTIONS ANSWERED	*Robert Chartham* 35p
☐ 552 09151 0	THE DRAGON AND THE PHOENIX	*Eric Chou* 50p
☐ 552 98959 8	THE ISLAND RACE Vol. 1	*Winston S. Churchill* 125p
☐ 552 98959 5	THE ISLAND RACE Vol. 2	*Winston S. Churchill* 125p
☐ 552 08800 5	CHARIOTS OF THE GODS? (illustrated)	*Eric von Daniken* 35p
☐ 552 09073 2	RETURN TO THE STARS (illustrated)	*Eric von Daniken* 40p
☐ 552 09135 9	THE HUMAN ANIMAL (illustrated)	*Hans Hass* 40p
☐ 552 07400 4	MY LIFE AND LOVES	*Frank Harris* 65p
☐ 552 98748 4	MAKING LOVE (Photographs)	*Walter Hartford* 85p
☐ 552 09062 X	THE SENSUOUS MAN	*'M'* 35p
☐ 555 08069 1	THE OTHER VICTORIANS	*Steven Marcus* 50p
☐ 525 09116 2	A BRITISH SURVEY IN FEMALE SEXUALITY	*Sandra McDermott* 40p
☐ 552 08010 1	THE NAKED APE	*Desmond Morris* 30p
☐ 552 09232 0	SECRET OF THE ANDES	*Brother Philip* 30p
☐ 552 09016 6	GOLF TACTICS	*Arnold Palmer* 45p
☐ 552 09230 4	BUGLES AND A TIGER	*John Masters* 40p
☐ 552 08880 3	THE THIRTEENTH CANDLE	*T. Lobsang Rampa* 25p
☐ 552 09266 5	ANY WOMAN CAN	*David R. Reuben M.D.* 50p
☐ 552 09044 1	SEX ENERGY	*Robert S. de Ropp* 35p
☐ 552 09250 9	THE MANIPULATED MAN	*Esther Vilar* 35p
☐ 552 09145 6	THE NYMPHO AND OTHER MANIACS	*Irving Wallace* 40p

Western

Crime

All these books are available at your bookshop or newsagent: or can be ordered direct from the publishers. Just tick the titles you want and fill in the form below.

CORGI BOOKS, Cash Sales Department, P.O. Box 11, Falmouth, Cornwall.
Please send cheque or postal order. No currency, and allow 6p per book to cover the cost of postage and packing in the U.K. and overseas.

NAME ....

ADDRESS ....

(JULY 73) ....